the melancholy chasers

Ray Bradbury's characters are his agents in the enterprise of melancholy-chasing. Some of them are strange and wonderful and golden-eyed; one is middle-aged and sad and thwarted in his romantic endeavors by a peculiar little hole in his head; another, a huge and terrifying dragon with a funny whistle.

After you've read the stories and met the people and caught your breath, you will agree with the critic who said: "Ray Bradbury is a great and unusual talent."

Books by Ray Bradbury

Published by Bantam Books

a medicine
for
melancholy
by ray
bradbury

YOUR ASSURANCE OF QUALITY · NEW YORK · BANTAM BOOKS ·

*This low-priced Bantam Book
has been completely reset in a type face
designed for easy reading, and was
printed from new plates. It contains the complete
text of the original hard-cover edition.*
NOT ONE WORD HAS BEEN OMITTED.

A MEDICINE FOR MELANCHOLY

*A Bantam Book / published by arrangement with
Doubleday and Company, Inc.*

PRINTING HISTORY
*Doubleday edition published February 1959
Bantam edition published April 1960
2nd printing ... September 1963
3rd printing
4th printing
5th printing*

THE WONDERFUL ICE CREAM SUIT, originally published in The
Saturday Evening Post as THE MAGIC WHITE SUIT. Copyright ©
1958 by The Curtis Publishing Company.

THE TOWN WHERE NO ONE GOT OFF, originally published in Ellery
Queen's Mystery Magazine. Copyright © 1958 by Davis Publica-
tions, Inc.

ALL SUMMER IN A DAY and ICARUS MONTGOLFIER WRIGHT, originally
published in Fantasy & Science Fiction Magazine.

THE FIRST NIGHT OF LENT and IN A SEASON OF CALM WEATHER,
originally published in Playboy. Copyright © 1956 by HMH Publishing Co., Inc.

THE GREAT COLLISION OF MONDAY LAST, originally published in
Argosy, London, as COLLISION OF MONDAY.

THE HEADPIECE, originally published in Lilliput, London.

A SCENT OF SARSAPARILLA and THE STRAWBERRY WINDOW, originally
published in Star Science Fiction Stories #1 and #3 respectively,
published by Ballantine Books, Inc.

THE SMILE, originally published in Fantastic Magazine.

THE LITTLE MICE, originally published in Escapade as THE MICE.

THE END OF THE BEGINNING, originally published in Maclean's
Magazine as NEXT STOP: THE STARS.

DARK THEY WERE AND GOLDEN-EYED, originally published in Thrilling Wonder Stories as THE NAMING OF NAMES. Copyright 1949 by
Standard Magazines, Inc.

For Dad,

whose love, very late in life, surprised his son.

And for Bernard Berenson *and* Nicky Mariano,

who gave me a new world.

Contents

*In
a
Season
of
Calm
Weather*

George and Alice Smith detrained at Biarritz one summer noon and in an hour had run through their hotel onto the beach into the ocean and back out to bake upon the sand.

To see George Smith sprawled burning there, you'd think him only a tourist flown fresh as iced lettuce to Europe and soon to be transshipped home. But here was a man who loved art more than life itself.

"There . . ." George Smith sighed. Another ounce of perspiration trickled down his chest. Boil out the Ohio tap water, he thought, then drink down the best Bordeaux. Silt your blood with rich French sediment so you'll see with native eyes!

Why? Why eat, breathe, drink everything French? So that, given time, he might really begin to understand the genius of one man.

His mouth moved, forming a name.

"George?" His wife loomed over him. "I know what you've been thinking. I can read your lips."

He lay perfectly still, waiting.

"And?"

"Picasso," she said.

He winced. Someday she would learn to pronounce that name.

1

"Please," she said. "Relax. I know you heard the rumor this morning, but you should see your eyes—your tic is back. All right, Picasso's here, down the coast a few miles away, visiting friends in some small fishing town. But you must forget it or our vacation's ruined."

"I wish I'd never heard the rumor," he said honestly.

"If only," she said, "you liked other painters."

Others? Yes, there were others. He could breakfast most congenially on Caravaggio still lifes of autumn pears and midnight plums. For lunch: those fire-squirting, thick-wormed Van Gogh sunflowers, those blooms a blind man might read with one rush of scorched fingers down fiery canvas. But the great feast? The paintings he saved his palate for? There, filling the horizon like Neptune risen, crowned with limeweed, alabaster, coral, paint-brushes clenched like tridents in horn-nailed fists, and with fishtail vast enough to fluke summer showers out over all Gibraltar—who else but the creator of *Girl Before a Mirror* and *Guernica*?

"Alice," he said patiently, "how can I explain? Coming down on the train, I thought, Good lord, it's *all* Picasso country!"

But was it really? he wondered. The sky, the land, the people, the flushed pink bricks here, scrolled electric-blue ironwork balconies there, a mandolin ripe as a fruit in some man's thousand fingerprinting hands, billboard tatters blowing like confetti in night winds—how much was Picasso, how much George Smith staring round the world with wild Picasso eyes? He despaired of answering. That old man had distilled turpentines and linseed oil so thoroughly through George Smith that they shaped his being, all Blue Period at twilight, all Rose Period at dawn.

"I keep thinking," he said aloud, "if we saved our money . . ."

"We'll never have five thousand dollars."

"I know," he said quietly. "But it's nice thinking we might bring it off someday. Wouldn't it be great to just step up to him, say 'Pablo, here's five thousand! Give us the sea, the sand, that sky, or any old thing you want, we'll be happy . . .' "

After a moment his wife touched his arm.

"I think you'd better go in the water now," she said.

"Yes," he said. "I'd better do just that."

White fire showered up when he cut the water.

During the afternoon George Smith came out and went into the ocean with the vast spilling motions of now warm, now cool people who at last, with the sun's decline, their bodies all lobster colors and colors of broiled squab and guinea hen, trudged for their wedding-cake hotels.

The beach lay deserted for endless mile on mile save for two people. One was George Smith, towel over shoulder, out for a last devotional.

Far along the shore another shorter, square-cut man walked alone in the tranquil weather. He was deeper-tanned, his close-shaven head dyed almost mahogany by the sun, and his eyes were clear and bright as water in his face.

So the shore-line stage was set, and in a few minutes the two men would meet. And once again Fate fixed the scales for shocks and surprises, arrivals and departures. And all the while these two solitary strollers did not for a moment think on coincidence, that unswum stream which lingers at man's elbow with every crowd in every town. Nor did they ponder the fact that if man dares dip into that stream he grabs a wonder in each hand. Like most, they shrugged at such folly and stayed well up the bank lest Fate should shove them in.

The stranger stood alone. Glancing about, he saw his aloneness, saw the waters of the lovely bay, saw the sun sliding down the late colors of the day, and then, half turning, spied a small wooden object on the sand. It was no more than the slender stick from a lime ice cream delicacy long since melted away. Smiling, he picked the stick up. With another glance around to reinsure his solitude, the man stooped again and, holding the stick gently, with light sweeps of his hand began to do the one thing in all the world he knew best how to do.

He began to draw incredible figures along the sand.

He sketched one figure and then moved over and, still looking down, completely focused on his work now, drew a second and a third figure, and after that a fourth and a fifth and a sixth.

George Smith, printing the shore line with his feet, gazed here, gazed there, and then saw the man ahead. George Smith, drawing nearer, saw that the man, deeply tanned, was bending down. Nearer yet, and it was obvious what the man was up to. George Smith chuckled. Of course, of course . . . Alone on the beach this man— how old? Sixty-five? Seventy?—was scribbling and doodling away. How the sand flew! How the wild portraits flung themselves out there on the shore! How . . .

George Smith took one more step and stopped, very still.

The stranger was drawing and drawing and did not seem to sense that anyone stood immediately behind him and the world of his drawings in the sand. By now he was so deeply enchanted with his solitudinous creation that depth bombs set off in the bay might not have stopped his flying hand nor turned him round.

George Smith looked down at the sand. And after a long while, looking, he began to tremble.

For there on the flat shore were pictures of Grecian lions and Mediterranean goats and maidens with flesh of sand like powdered gold and satyrs piping on hand-carved horns and children dancing, strewing flowers along and along the beach with lambs gamboling after, and musicians skipping to their harps and lyres and unicorns racing youths toward distant meadows, woodlands, ruined temples, and volcanoes. Along the shore in a never-broken line, the hand, the wooden stylus of this man, bent down in fever and raining perspiration, scribbled, ribboned, looped around over and up, across, in, out, stitched, whispered, stayed, then hurried on as if this traveling bacchanal must flourish to its end before the sun was put out by the sea. Twenty, thirty yards or more the nymphs and dryads and summer founts sprang up in unraveled hieroglyphs. And the sand in the dying light was the color of molten copper on which was now slashed a message that any man in any time might read and savor down the years. Everything whirled and poised in its own wind and gravity. Now wine was being crushed from under the grape-blooded feet of dancing vintners' daughters, now steaming seas gave birth to coin-sheathed monsters while flowered kites strewed scent on blowing clouds . . . now . . . now . . . now . . .

The artist stopped.

George Smith drew back and stood away.

The artist glanced up, surprised to find someone so near. Then he simply stood there, looking from George Smith to his own creations flung like idle footprints down the way. He smiled at last and shrugged as if to say, Look what I've done; see what a child? You will forgive me, won't you? One day or another we are all fools . . . You too, perhaps? So allow an old fool this, eh? Good! Good!

But George Smith could only look at the little man with the sun-dark skin and the clear sharp eyes and say the man's name once, in a whisper, to himself.

They stood thus for perhaps another five seconds. George Smith staring at the sand-frieze, and the artist watching George Smith with amused curiosity. George Smith opened his mouth, closed it, put out his hand, took it back. He stepped toward the pictures, stepped away. Then he moved along the line of figures, like a man viewing a precious series of marbles cast up from some ancient ruin on the shore. His eyes did not blink, his hand wanted to touch but did not dare to touch. He wanted to run but did not run.

He looked suddenly at the hotel. Run, yes! Run! What? Grab a shovel, dig, excavate, save a chunk of this all-too-crumbling sand? Find a repairman, race him back here with plaster of Paris to cast a mold of some small fragile part of these? No, no. Silly, silly. Or . . . ? His eyes flicked to his hotel window. The camera! Run, get it, get back, and hurry along the shore, clicking, changing film, clicking, until . . .

George Smith whirled to face the sun. It burned faintly on his face; his eyes were two small fires from it. The sun was half underwater, and as he watched it sank the rest of the way in a matter of seconds.

The artist had drawn nearer and now was gazing into George Smith's face with great friendliness, as if he were guessing every thought. Now he was nodding his head in a little bow. Now the ice cream stick had fallen casually from his fingers. Now he was saying good night, good night. Now he was gone, walking back down the beach toward the south.

George Smith stood looking after him. After a full minute he did the only thing he could possibly do. He started at the beginning of the fantastic frieze of satyrs and fauns and wine-dipped maidens and prancing unicorns and piping youths and he walked slowly along the shore. He walked a long way, looking down at the free-running bacchanal. And when he came to the end of the animals and men he turned around and started back in the other direction, just staring down as if he had lost something and did not quite know where to find it. He kept on doing this until there was no more light in the sky or on the sand to see by.

He sat down at the supper table.

"You're late," said his wife. "I just had to come down alone. I'm ravenous."

"That's all right," he said.

"Anything interesting happen on your walk?" she asked.

"No," he said.

"You look funny; George, you didn't swim out too far, did you, and almost drown? I can tell by your face. You *did* swim out too far, didn't you?"

"Yes," he said.

"Well," she said, watching him closely. "Don't ever do that again. Now—what'll you have?"

He picked up the menu and started to read it and stopped suddenly.

"What's wrong?" asked his wife.

He turned his head and shut his eyes for a moment.

"Listen."

She listened.

"I don't hear anything," she said.

"Don't you?"

"No. What is it?"

"Just the tide," he said after a while, sitting there, his eyes still shut. "Just the tide coming in."

The
Dragon

The night blew in the short grass on the moor; there was
no other motion. It had been years since a single bird
had flown by in the great blind shell of sky. Long ago a
few small stones had simulated life when they crumbled
and fell into dust. Now only the night moved in the
souls of the two men bent by their lonely fire in the wilderness; darkness pumped quietly in their veins and
ticked silently in their temples and their wrists.

Firelight fled up and down their wild faces and welled
in their eyes in orange tatters. They listened to each other's faint, cool breathing and the lizard blink of their
eyelids. At last, one man poked the fire with his sword.

"Don't, idiot; you'll give us away!"

"No matter," said the second man. "The dragon can
smell us miles off anyway. God's breath, it's cold. I wish
I was back at the castle."

"It's death, not sleep, we're after. . . ."

"Why? Why? The dragon never sets foot in the town!"

"Quiet, fool! He eats men traveling alone from our
town to the next!"

"Let them be eaten and let us get home!"

"Wait now; listen!"

The two men froze.

They waited a long time, but there was only the shake

7

of their horses' nervous skin like black velvet tambou-
rines jingling the silver stirrup buckles, softly, softly.

"Ah." The second man sighed. "What a land of night-
mares. Everything happens here. Someone blows out the
sun; it's night. And then, and *then,* oh, God, listen! This
dragon, they say his eyes are fire. His breath a white gas;
you can see him burn across the dark lands. He runs
with sulfur and thunder and kindles the grass. Sheep panic
and die insane. Women deliver forth monsters. The dragon's fury is such that tower walls shake back to dust. His
victims, at sunrise, are strewn hither thither on the hills.
How many knights, I ask, have gone for this monster and
failed, even as we shall fail?"

"Enough of that!"

"More than enough! Out here in this desolation I cannot tell what year this is!"

"Nine hundred years since the Nativity."

"No, no," whispered the second man, eyes shut. "On
this moor is no Time, is only Forever. I feel if I ran
back on the road the town would be gone, the people yet
unborn, things changed, the castles unquarried from the
rocks, the timbers still uncut from the forests; don't ask
how I know; the moor knows and tells me. And here we
sit alone in the land of the fire dragon, God save us!"

"Be you afraid, then gird on your armor!"

"What use? The dragon runs from nowhere; we cannot
guess its home. It vanishes in fog; we know not where it
goes. Aye, on with our armor, we'll die well dressed."

Half into his silver corselet, the second man stopped
again and turned his head.

Across the dim country, full of night and nothingness
from the heart of the moor itself, the wind sprang full of
dust from clocks that used dust for telling time. There
were black suns burning in the heart of this new wind and
a million burnt leaves shaken from some autumn tree beyond the horizon. This wind melted landscapes, length-
ened bones like white wax, made the blood roil and thick-
en to a muddy deposit in the brain. The wind was a thousand souls dying and all time confused and in transit. It
was a fog inside of a mist inside of a darkness, and this
place was no man's place and there was no year or hour
at all, but only these men in a faceless emptiness of sud-

den frost, storm and white thunder which moved behind
the great falling pane of green glass that was the lightning.
A squall of rain drenched the turf; all faded away until
there was unbreathing hush and the two men waiting
alone with their warmth in a cool season.

"There," whispered the first man. "Oh, *there* . . ."

Miles off, rushing with a great chant and a roar—the
dragon.

In silence the men buckled on their armor and mounted
their horses. The midnight wilderness was split by a monstrous gushing as the dragon roared nearer, nearer; its
flashing yellow glare spurted above a hill and then, fold on
fold of dark body, distantly seen, therefore indistinct,
flowed over that hill and plunged vanishing into a valley.

"Quick!"

They spurred their horses forward to a small hollow.

"This is where it passes!"

They seized their lances with mailed fists and blinded
their horses by flipping the visors down over their eyes.

"Lord!"

"Yes, let us use His name."

On the instant, the dragon rounded a hill. Its monstrous
amber eye fed on them, fired their armor in red glints
and glitters. With a terrible wailing cry and a grinding
rush it flung itself forward.

"Mercy, God!"

The lance struck under the unlidded yellow eye, buckled, tossed the man through the air. The dragon hit,
spilled him over, down, ground him under. Passing, the
black brunt of its shoulder smashed the remaining horse
and rider a hundred feet against the side of a boulder,
wailing, wailing, the dragon shrieking, the fire all about,
around, under it, a pink, yellow, orange sun-fire with great
soft plumes of blinding smoke.

"Did you *see* it?" cried a voice. "Just like I told you!"

"The same! The same! A knight in armor, by the Lord
Harry! We *hit* him!"

"You goin' to stop?"

"Did once; found nothing. Don't like to stop on this
moor. I get the willies. Got a *feel,* it has."

"But we hit *something!*"

"Gave him plenty of whistle; chap wouldn't budge!"

A steaming blast cut the mist aside.

"We'll make Stokely on time. More coal, eh, Fred?"

Another whistle shook dew from the empty sky. The night train, in fire and fury, shot through a gully, up a rise, and vanished away over cold earth toward the north, leaving black smoke and steam to dissolve in the numbed air minutes after it had passed and gone forever.

A
Medicine
for
Melancholy

(or: *The Sovereign Remedy Revealed!*)

"Send for some leeches; bleed her," said Doctor Gimp.

"She has no blood left!" cried Mrs. Wilkes. "Oh, Doctor, what ails our Camillia?"

"She's not right."

"Yes, yes?"

"She's poorly." The good doctor scowled.

"Go on, go on!"

"She's a fluttering candle flame, no doubt."

"Ah, Doctor Gimp," protested Mr. Wilkes. "You but tell us as you go out what we told you when you came in!"

"No, more! Give her these pills at dawn, high noon, and sunset. A sovereign remedy!"

"Damn, she's *stuffed* with sovereign remedies now!"

"Tut-tut! That's a shilling as I pass downstairs, sir."

"Go down and send the Devil up!" Mr. Wilkes shoved a coin in the good doctor's hand.

Whereupon the physician, wheezing, taking snuff, sneezing, stamped down into the swarming streets of London on a sloppy morn in the spring of 1762.

Mr. and Mrs. Wilkes turned to the bed where their sweet Camillia lay pale, thin, yes, but far from unlovely, with large wet lilac eyes, her hair a creek of gold upon her pillow.

11

"Oh," she almost wept. "What's to become of me? Since the start of spring, three weeks, I've been a ghost in my mirror; I frighten me. To think I'll die without seeing my twentieth birthday."

"Child," said the mother. "Where do you hurt?"

"My arms. My legs. My bosom. My head. How many doctors—six?—have turned me like a beef on a spit. No more. Please, let me pass away untouched."

"What a ghastly, what a mysterious illness," said the mother. "Oh, do something, Mr. Wilkes!"

"What?" asked Mr. Wilkes angrily. "She won't have the physician, the apothecary, or the priest!—and Amen to that!—they've wrung me dry! Shall I run in the street then and bring the Dustman up?"

"Yes," said a voice.

"What!" All three turned to stare.

They had quite forgotten her younger brother, Jamie, who stood picking his teeth at a far window, gazing serenely down into the drizzle and the loud rumbling of the town.

"Four hundred years ago," he said serenely, "it was tried, it worked. Don't bring the Dustman up, no, no. But let us hoist Camillia, cot and all, maneuver her downstairs, and set her up outside our door."

"Why? What for?"

"In a single hour"—Jamie's eyes jumped, counting—"a thousand folk rush by our gate. In one day, twenty thousand people run, hobble, or ride by. Each might eye my swooning sister, each count her teeth, pull her ear lobes, and all, all, mind you, would have a sovereign remedy to offer! One of them would just have to be right!"

"Ah," said Mr. Wilkes, stunned.

"Father!" said Jamie breathlessly. "Have you ever known one single man who didn't think he personally wrote *Materia Medica*? This green ointment for sour throat, that ox-salve for miasma or bloat? Right now, ten thousand self-appointed apothecaries sneak off down there, their wisdom lost to us!"

"Jamie boy, you're incredible!"

"Cease!" said Mrs. Wilkes. "No daughter of mine will be put on display in this or any street——"

"Fie, woman!" said Mr. Wilkes. "Camillia melts like

snow and you hesitate to move her from this hot room? Come, Jamie, lift the bed!"

"Camillia?" Mrs. Wilkes turned to her daughter.

"I may as well die in the open," said Camillia, "where a cool breeze might stir my locks as I . . ."

"Bosh!" said the father. "You'll not die. Jamie, heave! Ha! There! Out of the way, wife! Up, boy, *higher!*"

"Oh," cried Camillia faintly. "I fly, I *fly* . . . !"

Quite suddenly a blue sky opened over London. The population, surprised by the weather, hurried out into the streets, panicking for something to see, to do, to buy. Blind men sang, dogs jigged, clowns shuffled and tumbled, children chalked games and threw balls as if it were carnival time.

Down into all this, tottering, their veins bursting from their brows, Jamie and Mr. Wilkes carried Camillia like a lady Pope sailing high in her sedan-chair cot, eyes clenched shut, praying.

"Careful!" screamed Mrs. Wilkes. "Ah, she's dead! No. There. Put her down. Easy . . ."

And at last the bed was tilted against the house front so that the River of Humanity surging by could see Camillia, a large pale Bartolemy Doll put out like a prize in the sun.

"Fetch a quill, ink, paper, lad," said the father. "I'll make notes as to symptoms spoken of and remedies offered this day. Tonight we'll average them out. Now——"

But already a man in the passing crowd had fixed Camillia with a sharp eye.

"She's sick!" he said.

"Ah," said Mr. Wilkes, gleefully. "It begins. The quill, boy. There. Go on, sir!"

"She's not well." The man scowled. "She does poorly."

"Does poorly——" Mr. Wilkes wrote, then froze. "Sir?" He looked up suspiciously. "Are you a physician?"

"I am, sir."

"I *thought* I knew the words! Jamie, take my cane, drive him off! Go, sir, be gone!"

But the man hastened off, cursing, mightily exasperated.

"She's not well, she does poorly . . . pah!" mimicked

Mr. Wilkes, but stopped. For now a woman, tall and
gaunt as a specter fresh risen from the tomb, was pointing a finger at Camillia Wilkes.

"Vapors," she intoned.

"Vapors," wrote Mr. Wilkes, pleased.

"Lung-flux," chanted the woman.

"Lung-flux!" Mr. Wilkes wrote, beaming. "Now, that's
more *like* it!"

"A medicine for melancholy is needed," said the
woman palely. "Be there mummy ground to medicine in
your house? The best mummies are: Egyptian, Arabian,
Hirasphatos, Libyan, all of great use in magnetic disorders. Ask for me, the Gypsy, at the Flodden Road. I
sell stone parsley, male frankincense——"

"Flodden Road, stone parsley—slower, woman!"

"Opobalsam, pontic valerian——"

"Wait, woman! Opobalsam, yes! Jamie, stop her!"

But the woman, naming medicines, glided on.

A girl, no more than seventeen, walked up now and
stared at Camillia Wilkes.

"She——"

"One moment!" Mr. Wilkes scribbled feverishly. "—
magnetic disorders—pontic valerian—drat! Well, young
girl, now. What do you see in my daughter's face? You
fix her with your gaze, you hardly breathe. So?"

"She——" The strange girl searched deep into Camillia's eyes, flushed, and stammered. "She suffers from
. . . from . . ."

"Spit it out!"

"She . . . she . . . oh!"

And the girl, with a last look of deepest sympathy,
darted off through the crowd.

"Silly girl!"

"No, Papa," murmured Camillia, eyes wide. "Not
silly. She *saw*. She *knew*. Oh, Jamie, run fetch her, make
her tell!"

"No, she offered nothing! Whereas, the Gypsy, see her
list!"

"I know it, Papa." Camillia, paler, shut her eyes.

Someone cleared his throat.

A butcher, his apron a scarlet battleground, stood
bristling his fierce mustaches there.

"I have seen cows with this look," he said. "I have saved them with brandy and three new eggs. In winter I have saved myself with the same elixir——"

"My daughter is no cow, sir!" Mr. Wilkes threw down his quill. "Nor is she a butcher, nor is it January! Step back, sir, others wait!"

And indeed, now a vast crowd clamored, drawn by the others, aching to advise their favorite swig, recommend some country site where it rained less and shone more sun than in all England or your South of France. Old men and women, especial doctors as all the aged are, clashed by each other in bristles of canes, in phalanxes of crutches and hobble sticks.

"Back!" cried Mrs. Wilkes, alarmed. "They'll crush my daughter like a spring berry!"

"Stand off!" Jamie seized canes and crutches and threw them over the mob, which turned on itself to go seek their missing members.

"Father, I fail, I fail," gasped Camillia.

"Father!" cried Jamie. "There's but one way to stop this riot! Charge them! Make them pay to give us their mind on this ailment!"

"Jamie, you are my son! Quick, boy, paint a sign! Listen, people! Tuppence! Queue up please, a line! Tuppence to speak your piece! Get your money out, yes! That's it. You, sir. You, madame. And you, sir. Now, my quill! Begin!"

The mob boiled in like a dark sea.

Camillia opened one eye and swooned again.

Sundown, the streets almost empty, only a few strollers now. Camillia moth-fluttered her eyelids at a familiar clinking jingle.

"Three hundred and ninety-nine, four hundred pennies!" Mr. Wilkes counted the last money into a bag held by his grinning son. "There!"

"It will buy me a fine black funeral coach," said the pale girl.

"Hush! Did you imagine, family, so many people, two hundred, would pay to give us their opinion?"

"Yes," said Mrs. Wilkes. "Wives, husbands, children, are deaf to each other. So people gladly pay to have

someone listen. Poor things, each today thought he and
he alone knew quinsy, dropsy, glanders, could tell the
slaver from the hives. So tonight we are rich and two
hundred people are happy, having unloaded their full
medical kit at our door."

"Gods, instead of quelling the riot, we had to drive
them off snapping like pups."

"Read us the list, Father," said Jamie, "of two hundred remedies. Which one is true?"

"I care not," whispered Camillia, sighing. "It grows
dark. My stomach is queasy from listening to the names!
May I be taken upstairs?"

"Yes, dear. Jamie, lift!"

"Please," said a voice.

Half-bent, the men looked up.

There stood a Dustman of no particular size or shape,
his face masked with soot from which shone water-blue
eyes and a white slot of an ivory smile. Dust sifted from
his sleeves and his pants as he moved, as he talked quietly,
nodding.

"I couldn't get through the mob earlier," he said, holding his dirty cap in his hands. "Now, going home, here I
am. Must I pay?"

"No, Dustman, you need not," said Camillia gently.

"Hold on——" protested Mr. Wilkes.

But Camilia gave him a soft look and he grew silent.

"Thank you, ma'am." The Dustman's smile flashed like
warm sunlight in the growing dusk. "I have but one advice."

He gazed at Camillia. She gazed at him.

"Be this Saint Bosco's Eve, sir, ma'am?"

"Who knows? Not *me*, sir!" said Mr. Wilkes.

"I think it *is* Saint Bosco's Eve, sir. Also, it is the night
of the Full Moon. So," said the Dustman humbly, unable
to take his eyes from the lovely haunted girl, "you must
leave your daughter out in the light of that rising moon."

"Out under the moon!" said Mrs. Wilkes.

"Doesn't that make the lunatic?" asked Jamie.

"Beg pardon, sir." The Dustman bowed. "But the full
moon soothes all sick animal, be they human or plain
field beast. There is a serenity of color, a quietude of

touch, a sweet sculpturing of mind and body in full moonlight."

"It may rain——" said the mother uneasily.

"I swear," said the Dustman quickly. "My sister suffered this same swooning paleness. We set her like a potted lily out one spring night with the moon. She lives today in Sussex, the soul of reconstituted health!"

"Reconstituted! Moonlight! And will cost us not one penny of the four hundred we collected this day, Mother, Jamie, Camillia."

"No!" said Mrs. Wilkes. "I won't have it!"

"Mother," said Camillia.

She looked earnestly at the Dustman.

From his grimed face the Dustman gazed back, his smile like a little scimitar in the dark.

"Mother," said Camillia. "I feel it. The moon will cure me, it will, it will. . . ."

The mother sighed. "This is not my day, nor night. Let me kiss you for the last time, then. There."

And the mother went upstairs.

Now the Dustman backed off, bowing courteously to all.

"All night, now, remember, beneath the moon, not the slightest disturbance until dawn. Sleep well, young lady. Dream, and dream the best. Good night."

Soot was lost in soot; the man was gone.

Mr. Wilkes and Jamie kissed Camillia's brow.

"Father, Jamie," she said. "Don't worry."

And she was left alone to stare off where at a great distance she thought she saw a smile hung by itself in the dark blink off and on, then go round a corner, vanishing.

She waited for the rising of the moon.

Night in London, the voices growing drowsier in the inns, the slamming of doors, drunken farewells, clocks chiming. Camillia saw a cat like a woman stroll by in her furs, saw a woman like a cat stroll by, both wise, both Egyptian, both smelling of spice. Every quarter hour or so a voice drifted down from above:

"You all right, child?"

"Yes, Father."

"Camillia?"

"Mother, Jamie, I'm fine."

And at last. "Good night."

"Good night."

The last lights out. London asleep.

The moon rose.

And the higher the moon, the larger grew Camillia's eyes as she watched the alleys, the courts, the streets, until at last, at midnight, the moon moved over her to show her like a marble figure atop an ancient tomb.

A motion in darkness.

Camillia pricked her ears.

A faint melody sprang out on the air.

A man stood in the shadows of the court.

Camillia gasped.

The man stepped forth into moonlight, carrying a lute which he strummed softly. He was a man well-dressed, whose face was handsome and, now anyway, solemn.

"A troubadour," said Camillia aloud.

The man, his finger on his lips, moved slowly forward and soon stood by her cot.

"What are you doing out so late?" asked the girl, unafraid but not knowing why.

"A friend sent me to make you well." He touched the lute strings. They hummed sweetly. He was indeed handsome there in the silver light.

"That cannot be," she said, "for it was told me, the *moon* is my cure."

"And so it will be, maiden."

"What songs do you sing?"

"Songs of spring nights, aches and ailments without name. Shall I name your fever, maiden?"

"If you know it, yes."

"First, the symptoms: raging temperatures, sudden cold, heart fast then slow, storms of temper, then sweet calms, drunkenness from having sipped only well water, dizziness from being touched only *thus*——"

He touched her wrist, saw her melt toward delicious oblivion, drew back.

"Depressions, elations," he went on. "Dreams——"

"Stop!" she cried, enthralled. "You know me to the letter. Now, name my ailment!"

"I will." He pressed his lips to the palm of her hand so she quaked suddenly. "The name of the ailment is Camillia Wilkes."

"How strange." She shivered, her eyes glinting lilac fires. "Am I then my own affliction? How sick I make myself! Even now, feel my heart!"

"I feel it, so."

"My limbs, they burn with summer heat!"

"Yes. They scorch my fingers."

"But now, the night wind, see how I shudder, cold! I die, I swear it, I die!"

"I will not let you," he said quietly.

"Are you a doctor, then?"

"No, just your plain, your ordinary physician, like another who guessed your trouble this day. The girl who would have named it but ran off in the crowd."

"Yes, I saw in her eyes she knew what had seized me. But, now, my teeth chatter. And no extra blanket!"

"Give room, please. There. Let me see: two arms, two legs, head and body. I'm all here!"

"What, sir!"

"To warm you from the night, of course."

"How like a hearth! Oh, sir, sir, do I *know* you? Your name?"

Swiftly above her, his head shadowed hers. From it his merry clear-water eyes glowed as did his white ivory slot of a smile.

"Why, Bosco, of course," he said.

"Is there not a saint by that name?"

"Given an hour, you will call me so, yes."

His head bent closer. Thus sooted in shadow, she cried with joyous recognition to welcome her Dustman back.

"The world spins! I pass away! The cure, sweet Doctor, or all is lost!"

"The cure," he said. "And the cure is *this* . . ."

Somewhere, cats sang. A shoe, shot from a window, tipped them off a fence. Then all was silence and the moon . . .

"Shh . . ."

Dawn. Tiptoeing downstairs, Mr. and Mrs. Wilkes peered into their courtyard.

"Frozen stone dead from the terrible night, I *know* it!"

"No, wife, look! Alive! Roses in her cheeks! No, more! Peaches, persimmons! She glows all rosy-milky! Sweet Camillia, alive and well, made whole again!"

They bent by the slumbering girl.

"She smiles, she dreams; what's that she says?"

"The sovereign," sighed the girl, "remedy."

"What, what?"

The girl smiled again, a white smile, in her sleep.

"A medicine," she murmured, "for melancholy."

She opened her eyes.

"Oh, Mother, Father!"

"Daughter! Child! Come upstairs!"

"No." She took their hands, tenderly. "Mother? Father?"

"Yes?"

"No one will see. The sun but rises. Please. Dance with me."

They did not want to dance.

But, celebrating they knew not what, they did.

The
End
of
the
Beginning

He stopped the lawn mower in the middle of the yard, because he felt that the sun at just that moment had gone down and the stars come out. The fresh-cut grass that had showered his face and body died softly away. Yes, the stars were there, faint at first, but brightening in the clear desert sky. He heard the porch screen door tap shut and felt his wife watching him as he watched the night.

"Almost time," she said.

He nodded; he did not have to check his watch. In the passing moments he felt very old, then very young, very cold, then very warm, now this, now that. Suddenly he was miles away. He was his own son talking steadily, moving briskly to cover his pounding heart and the resurgent panics as he felt himself slip into fresh uniform, check food supplies, oxygen flasks, pressure helmet, space-suiting, and turn as every man on earth tonight turned, to gaze at the swiftly filling sky.

Then, quickly, he was back, once more the father of the son, hands gripped to the lawn-mower handle. His wife called, "Come sit on the porch."

"I've got to keep busy!"

She came down the steps and across the lawn. "Don't worry about Robert; he'll be all right."

"But it's all so new," he heard himself say. "It's never

21

been done before. Think of it—a manned rocket going up tonight to build the first space station. Good lord, it can't be done, it doesn't exist, there's no rocket, no proving ground, no take-off time, no technicians. For that matter, I don't even have a son named Bob. The whole thing's too much for me!"

"Then what are you doing out here, staring?"

He shook his head. "Well, late this morning, walking to the office, I heard someone laugh out loud. It shocked me, so I froze in the middle of the street. It was *me,* laughing! Why? Because finally I really *knew* what Bob was going to do tonight; at last I *believed* it. Holy is a word I never use, but that's how I felt stranded in all that traffic. Then, middle of the afternoon I caught myself humming. You know the song. 'A wheel in a wheel. Way in the middle of the air.' I laughed again. The space station, of course, I thought. The big wheel with hollow spokes where Bob'll live six or eight months, then get along to the moon. Walking home, I remembered more of the song. 'Little wheel run by faith, Big wheel run by the grace of God.' I wanted to jump, yell, and flame-out myself!"

His wife touched his arm. "If we stay out here, let's at least be comfortable."

They placed two wicker rockers in the center of the lawn and sat quietly as the stars dissolved out of darkness in pale crushings of rock salt strewn from horizon to horizon.

"Why," said his wife, at last, "it's like waiting for the fireworks at Sisley Field every year."

"Bigger crowd tonight . . ."

"I keep thinking—a billion people watching the sky right now, their mouths all open at the same time."

They waited, feeling the earth move under their chairs.

"What time is it now?"

"Eleven minutes to eight."

"You're always right; there must be a clock in your head."

"I can't be wrong tonight. I'll be able to tell you one second before they blast off. Look! The ten-minute warning!"

On the western sky they saw four crimson flares open

out, float shimmering down the wind above the desert, then sink silently to the extinguishing earth.

In the new darkness the husband and wife did not rock in their chairs.

After a while he said, "Eight minutes." A pause. "Seven minutes." What seemed a much longer pause. "Six . . ."

His wife, her head back, studied the stars immediately above her and murmured, "Why?" She closed her eyes. "Why the rockets, why tonight? Why all this? I'd like to know."

He examined her face, pale in the vast powdering light of the Milky Way. He felt the stirring of an answer, but let his wife continue.

"I mean it's not that old thing again, is it, when people asked why men climbed Mt. Everest and they said, 'Because it's there'? I never understood. That was no answer to me."

Five minutes, he thought. Time ticking . . . his wrist watch . . . a wheel in a wheel . . . little wheel run by . . . big wheel run by . . . way in the middle of . . . four minutes! . . . The men snug in the rocket by now, the hive, the control board flickering with light. . . .

His lips moved.

"All I know is it's really the end of the beginning. The Stone Age, Bronze Age, Iron Age; from now on we'll lump all those together under one big name for when we walked on Earth and heard the birds at morning and cried with envy. Maybe we'll call it the Earth Age, or maybe the Age of Gravity. Millions of years we fought gravity. When we were amoebas and fish we struggled to get out of the sea without gravity crushing us. Once safe on the shore we fought to stand upright without gravity breaking our new invention, the spine, tried to walk without stumbling, run without falling. A billion years Gravity kept us home, mocked us with wind and clouds, cabbage moths and locusts. That's what's so god-awful big about tonight . . . it's the end of old man Gravity and the age we'll remember him by, for once and all. I don't know where they'll divide the ages, at the Persians, who dreamt of flying carpets, or the Chinese, who all unknowing celebrated birthdays and New Years with strung ladyfingers and high skyrockets, or some minute, some incredible second in the next hour. But we're in at the end of a billion years trying, the end of something long and to us humans, anyway, honorable."

Three minutes . . . two minutes fifty-nine seconds . . . two minutes fifty-eight seconds . . .

"But," said his wife, "I still don't know why."

Two minutes, he thought. *Ready? Ready? Ready?* The far radio voice calling. *Ready! Ready! Ready!* The quick, faint replies from the humming rocket. *Check! Check! Check!*

Tonight, he thought, even if we fail with this first, we'll send a second and a third ship and move on out to all the planets and later, all the stars. We'll just keep going until the big words like immortal and forever take on meaning. Big words, yes, that's what we want. Continuity. Since our tongues first moved in our mouths we've asked, What does it all mean? No other question made sense, with death breathing down our necks. But just let us settle in on ten thousand worlds spinning around ten thousand alien suns and the question will fade away. Man will be endless and infinite, even as space is endless and infinite. Man will go on, as space goes on, forever. Individuals will die as always, but our history will reach as far as we'll ever need to see into the future, and with the knowledge of our survival for all time to come, we'll know security and thus the answer we've always searched for. Gifted with life, the least we can do is preserve and pass on the gift to infinity. That's a goal worth shooting for.

The wicker chairs whispered ever so softly on the grass.

One minute.

"One minute," he said aloud.

"Oh!" His wife moved suddenly to seize his hands. "I hope that Bob . . ."

"He'll be all right!"

"Oh, God, take care . . ."

Thirty seconds.

"Watch now."

Fifteen, ten, five . . .

"Watch!"

Four, three, two, one.

"There! There! Oh, there, there!"

They both cried out. They both stood. The chairs toppled back, fell flat on the lawn. The man and his wife
swayed, their hands struggled to find each other, grip,
hold. They saw the brightening color in the sky and, ten
seconds later, the great uprising comet burn the air, put
out the stars, and rush away in fire flight to become another star in the returning profusion of the Milky Way.
The man and wife held each other as if they had stumbled
on the rim of an incredible cliff that faced an abyss so
deep and dark there seemed no end to it. Staring up, they
heard themselves sobbing and crying. Only after a long
time were they able to speak.

"It got away, it did, *didn't* it?"

"Yes . . ."

"It's all right, isn't it?"

"Yes . . . yes . . ."

"It didn't fall back . . . ?"

"No, no, it's all right, Bob's all right, it's all right."

They stood away from each other at last.

He touched his face with his hand and looked at his
wet fingers. "I'll be damned," he said, "I'll be damned."

They waited another five and then ten minutes until the
darkness in their heads, the retina, ached with a million
specks of fiery salt. Then they had to close their eyes.

"Well," she said, "now let's go in."

He could not move. Only his hand reached a long way
out by itself to find the lawn-mower handle. He saw what
his hand had done and said, "There's just a little more to
do. . . ."

"But you can't see."

"Well enough," he said. "I must finish this. Then we'll
sit on the porch awhile before we turn in."

He helped her put the chairs on the porch and sat her
down and then walked back out to put his hands on the
guide bar of the lawn mower. The lawn mower. A wheel
in a wheel. A simple machine which you held in your
hands, which you sent on ahead with a rush and a clatter
while you walked behind with your quiet philosophy.
Racket, followed by warm silence. Whirling wheel, then
soft footfall of thought.

I'm a billion years old, he told himself; I'm one minute

old. I'm one inch, no, ten thousand *miles*, tall. I look down and can't see my feet they're so far off and gone away below.

He moved the lawn mower. The grass showering up fell softly around him; he relished and savored it and felt that he was all mankind bathing at last in the fresh waters of the fountain of youth.

Thus bathed, he remembered the song again about the wheels and the faith and the grace of God being way up there in the middle of the sky where that single star, among a million motionless stars, dared to move and keep on moving.

Then he finished cutting the grass.

The
Wonderful
Ice
Cream
Suit

It was summer twilight in the city, and out front of the quiet-clicking pool hall three young Mexican-American men breathed the warm air and looked around at the world. Sometimes they talked and sometimes they said nothing at all but watched the cars glide by like black panthers on the hot asphalt or saw trolleys loom up like thunderstorms, scatter lightning, and rumble away into silence.

"Hey," sighed Martínez at last. He was the youngest, the most sweetly sad of the three. "It's a swell night, huh? Swell."

As he observed the world it moved very close and then drifted away and then came close again. People, brushing by, were suddenly across the street. Buildings five miles away suddenly leaned over him. But most of the time everything—people, cars, and buildings—stayed way out on the edge of the world and could not be touched. On this quiet warm summer evening Martínez's face was cold.

"Nights like this you wish . . . lots of things."

"Wishing," said the second man, Villanazul, a man who shouted books out loud in his room but spoke only in whispers on the street. "Wishing is the useless pastime of the unemployed."

27

"Unemployed?" cried Vamenos, the unshaven. "Listen to him! We got no jobs, no money!"

"So," said Martínez, "we got no friends."

"True." Villanazul gazed off toward the green plaza where the palm trees swayed in the soft night wind. "Do you know what I wish? I wish to go into that plaza and speak among the businessmen who gather there nights to talk big talk. But dressed as I am, poor as I am, who would listen? So, Martínez, we have each other. The friendship of the poor is real friendship. We——"

But now a handsome young Mexican with a fine thin mustache strolled by. And on each of his careless arms hung a laughing woman.

"Madre mía!" Martínez slapped his own brow. "How does that one rate *two* friends?"

"It's his nice new white summer suit." Vamenos chewed a black thumbnail. "He looks sharp."

Martínez leaned out to watch the three people moving away, and then at the tenement across the street, in one fourth-floor window of which, far above, a beautiful girl leaned out, her dark hair faintly stirred by the wind. She had been there forever, which was to say for six weeks. He had nodded, he had raised a hand, he had smiled, he had blinked rapidly, he had even bowed to her, on the street, in the hall when visiting friends, in the park, downtown. Even now, he put his hand up from his waist and moved his fingers. But all the lovely girl did was let the summer wind stir her dark hair. He did not exist. He was nothing.

"Madre mía!" He looked away and down the street where the man walked his two friends around a corner. "Oh, if just I had one suit, one! I wouldn't need money if I *looked* okay."

"I hesitate to suggest," said Villanazul, "that you see Gómez. But he's been talking some crazy talk for a month now about clothes. I keep on saying I'll be in on it to make him go away. That Gómez."

"Friend," said a quiet voice.

"Gómez!" Everyone turned to stare.

Smiling strangely, Gómez pulled forth an endless thin yellow ribbon which fluttered and swirled on the summer air.

"Gómez," said Martínez, "what you doing with that tape measure?"

Gómez beamed. "Measuring people's skeletons."

"Skeletons!"

"Hold on." Gómez squinted at Martínez. *"Caramba!* Where you *been* all my life! Let's try *you!"*

Martínez saw his arm seized and taped, his leg measured, his chest encircled.

"Hold still!" cried Gómez. "Arm—perfect. Leg—chest —*perfecto!* Now quick, the height! There! Yes! Five foot five! You're in! Shake!" Pumping Martínez's hand, he stopped suddenly. "Wait. You got . . . ten bucks?"

"I have!" Vamenos waved some grimy bills. "Gómez, measure me!"

"All I got left in the world is nine dollars and ninety-two cents." Martínez searched his pockets. "That's enough for a new suit? Why?"

"Why? Because you got the right skeleton, that's why!"

"Señor Gómez, I don't hardly know you——"

"Know me? You're going to live with me! Come on!"

Gómez vanished into the poolroom. Martínez, escorted by the polite Villanazul, pushed by an eager Vamenos, found himself inside.

"Domínguez!" said Gómez.

Domínguez, at a wall telephone, winked at them. A woman's voice squeaked on the receiver.

"Manulo!" said Gómez.

Manulo, a wine bottle tilted bubbling to his mouth, turned.

Gómez pointed at Martínez.

"At last we found our fifth volunteer!"

Domínguez said, "I got a date, don't bother me——" and stopped. The receiver slipped from his fingers. His little black telephone book full of fine names and numbers went quickly back into his pocket. "Gómez, you——?"

"Yes, yes! Your money, now! *Ándale!"*

The woman's voice sizzled on the dangling phone.

Domínguez glanced at it uneasily.

Manulo considered the empty wine bottle in his hand and the liquor-store sign across the street.

Then very reluctantly both men laid ten dollars each on the green velvet pool table.

Villanazul, amazed, did likewise, as did Gómez, nudging Martínez. Martínez counted out his wrinkled bills and change. Gómez flourished the money like a royal flush.

"Fifty bucks! The suit costs sixty! All we need is ten bucks!"

"Wait," said Martínez. "Gómez, are we talking about *one* suit? *Uno?*"

"Uno!" Gómez raised a finger. "One wonderful white ice cream summer suit! White, white as the August moon!"

"But who will own this one suit?"

"Me!" said Manulo.

"Me!" said Domínguez.

"Me!" said Villanazul.

"Me!" cried Gómez. *"And* you, Martínez. Men, let's show him. Line up!"

Villanazul, Manulo, Domínguez, and Gómez rushed to plant their backs against the poolroom wall.

"Martínez, you too, the other end, line up! Now, Vamenos, lay that billiard cue across our heads!"

"Sure, Gómez, sure!"

Martínez, in line, felt the cue tap his head and leaned out to see what was happening. "Ah!" he gasped.

The cue lay flat on all their heads, with no rise or fall, as Vamenos slid it along, grinning.

"We're all the same height!" said Martínez.

"The same!" Everyone laughed.

Gómez ran down the line, rustling the yellow tape measure here and there on the men so they laughed even more wildly.

"Sure!" he said. "It took a month, four weeks, mind you, to find four guys the same size and shape as me, a month of running around measuring. Sometimes I found guys with five-foot-five skeletons, sure, but all the meat on their bones was too much or not enough. Sometimes their bones were too long in the legs or too short in the arms. Boy, all the bones! I tell you! But now, five of us, same shoulders, chests, waists, arms, and as for weight? Men!"

Manulo, Domínguez, Villanazul, Gómez, and at last Martínez stepped onto the scales which flipped ink-stamped cards at them as Vamenos, still smiling wildly, fed pennies. Heart pounding, Martínez read the cards.

"One hundred thirty-five pounds . . . one thirty-six . . . one thirty-three . . . one thirty-four . . . one thirty-seven . . . a miracle!"

"No," said Villanazul simply, "Gómez."

They all smiled upon that genius who now circled them with his arms.

"Are we not fine?" he wondered. "All the same size, all the same dream—the suit. So each of us will look beautiful at least one night each week, eh?"

"I haven't looked beautiful in years," said Martínez. "The girls run away."

"They will run no more, they will freeze," said Gómez, "when they see you in the cool white summer ice cream suit."

"Gómez," said Villanazul, "just let me ask one thing."

"Of course, *compadre.*"

"When we get this nice new white ice cream summer suit, some night you're not going to put it on and walk down to the Greyhound bus in it and go live in El Paso for a year in it, are you?"

"Villanazul, Villanazul, how can you say that?"

"My eye sees and my tongue moves," said Villanazul. "How about the *Everybody Wins!* Punchboard Lotteries you ran and you kept running when nobody won? How about the United Chili Con Carne and Frijole Company you were going to organize and all that ever happened was the rent ran out on a two-by-four office?"

"The errors of a child now grown," said Gómez. "Enough! In this hot weather someone may buy the special suit that is made just for us that stands waiting in the window of SHUMWAY'S SUNSHINE SUITS! We have fifty dollars. Now we need just one more skeleton!"

Martínez saw the men peer around the pool hall. He looked where they looked. He felt his eyes hurry past Vamenos, then come reluctantly back to examine his dirty shirt, his huge nicotined fingers.

"Me!" Vamenos burst out at last. "My skeleton, measure it, it's great! Sure, my hands are big, and my arms, from digging ditches! But——"

Just then Martínez heard passing on the sidewalk

outside that same terrible man with his two girls, all laughing together.

He saw anguish move like the shadow of a summer cloud on the faces of the other men in this poolroom.

Slowly Vamenos stepped onto the scales and dropped his penny. Eyes closed, he breathed a prayer.

"Madre mía, please . . ."

The machinery whirred; the card fell out. Vamenos opened his eyes.

"Look! One thirty-five pounds! Another miracle!"

The men stared at his right hand and the card, at his left hand and a soiled ten-dollar bill.

Gómez swayed. Sweating, he licked his lips. Then his hand shot out, seized the money.

"The clothing store! The suit! *Vamos!*"

Yelling, everyone ran from the poolroom.

The woman's voice was still squeaking on the abandoned telephone. Martínez, left behind, reached out and hung the voice up. In the silence he shook his head. *"Santos,* what a dream! Six men," he said, "one suit. What will come of this? Madness? Debauchery? Murder? But I go with God. Gómez, wait for me!"

Martínez was young. He ran fast.

Mr. Shumway, of SHUMWAY'S SUNSHINE SUITS, paused while adjusting a tie rack, aware of some subtle atmospheric change outside his establishment.

"Leo," he whispered to his assistant. "Look . . ."

Outside, one man, Gómez, strolled by, looking in. Two men, Manulo and Domínguez, hurried by, staring in. Three men, Villanazul, Martínez, and Vamenos, jostling shoulders, did the same.

"Leo." Mr. Shumway swallowed. "Call the police!"

Suddenly six men filled the doorway.

Martínez, crushed among them, his stomach slightly upset, his face feeling feverish, smiled so wildly at Leo that Leo let go the telephone.

"Hey," breathed Martínez, eyes wide. "There's a great suit over there!"

"No." Manulo touched a lapel. *"This* one!"

"There is only one suit in all the world!" said Gómez coldly. "Mr. Shumway, the ice cream white, size thirty-four, was in your window just an hour ago! It's gone! You didn't——"

"Sell it?" Mr. Shumway exhaled. "No, no. In the dressing room. It's still on the dummy."

Martínez did not know if he moved and moved the crowd or if the crowd moved and moved him. Suddenly they were all in motion. Mr. Shumway, running, tried to keep ahead of them.

"This way, gents. Now which of you . . . ?"

"All for one, one for all!" Martínez heard himself say, and laughed. "We'll all try it on!"

"All?" Mr. Shumway clutched at the booth curtain as if his shop were a steamship that had suddenly tilted in a great swell. He stared.

That's it, thought Martínez, look at our smiles. Now, look at the skeletons behind our smiles! Measure here, there, up, down, yes, do you *see?*

Mr. Shumway saw. He nodded. He shrugged.

"All!" He jerked the curtain. "There! Buy it, and I'll throw in the dummy free!"

Martínez peered quietly into the booth, his motion drawing the others to peer too.

The suit was there.

And it was white.

Martínez could not breathe. He did not want to. He did not need to. He was afraid his breath would melt the suit. It was enough, just looking.

But at last he took a great trembling breath and exhaled, whispering, "*Ay. Ay, caramba!*"

"It puts out my eyes," murmured Gómez.

"Mr. Shumway," Martínez heard Leo hissing. "Ain't it dangerous precedent, to sell it? I mean, what if everybody bought *one* suit for *six* people?"

"Leo," said Mr. Shumway, "you ever hear one single fifty-nine-dollar suit make so many people happy at the same time before?"

"Angels' wings," murmured Martínez. "The wings of white angels."

Martínez felt Mr. Shumway peering over his shoulder into the booth. The pale glow filled his eyes.

"You know something, Leo?" he said in awe. "That's a *suit!*"

Gómez, shouting, whistling, ran up to the third-floor landing and turned to wave to the others, who staggered, laughed, stopped, and had to sit down on the steps below.

"Tonight!" cried Gómez. "Tonight you move in with me, eh? Save rent as well as clothes, eh? Sure! Martínez, you got the suit?"

"Have I?" Martínez lifted the white gift-wrapped box high. "From us to us! *Ay-hah!*"

"Vamenos, you got the dummy?"

"Here!"

Vamenos, chewing an old cigar, scattering sparks, slipped. The dummy, falling, toppled, turned over twice, and banged down the stairs.

"Vamenos! Dumb! Clumsy!"

They seized the dummy from him. Stricken, Vamenos looked about as if he'd lost something.

Manulo snapped his fingers. "Hey, Vamenos, we got to celebrate! Go borrow some wine!"

Vamenos plunged downstairs in a whirl of sparks.

The others moved into the room with the suit, leaving Martínez in the hall to study Gómez's face.

"Gómez, you look sick."

"I am," said Gómez. "For what have I done?" He nodded to the shadows in the room working about the dummy. "I pick Domínguez, a devil with the women. All right. I pick Manulo, who drinks, yes, but who sings as sweet as a girl, eh? Okay. Villanazul reads books. You, you wash behind your ears. But then what do I do? Can I wait? No! I got to buy that suit! So the last guy I pick is a clumsy slob who has the right to wear *my* suit——" He stopped, confused. "Who gets to wear *our* suit one night a week, fall down in it, or not come in out of the rain in it! Why, why, why did I do it!"

"Gómez," whispered Villanazul from the room. "The suit is ready. Come see if it looks as good using *your* light bulb."

Gómez and Martínez entered.

And there on the dummy in the center of the room was the phosphorescent, the miraculously white-fired ghost with the incredible lapels, the precise stitching, the neat buttonholes. Standing with the white illumination of the suit upon his cheeks, Martínez suddenly felt he was in

church. White! White! It was white as the whitest vanilla
ice cream, as the bottled milk in tenement halls at dawn.
White as a winter cloud all alone in the moonlit sky late
at night. Seeing it here in the warm summer-night room
made their breath almost show on the air. Shutting his
eyes, he could see it printed on his lids. He knew what
color his dreams would be this night.

"White . . ." murmured Villanazul. "White as the snow
on that mountain near our town in Mexico, which is
called the Sleeping Woman."

"Say that again," said Gómez.

Villanazul, proud yet humble, was glad to repeat his
tribute.

". . . white as the snow on the mountain called———"

"I'm back!"

Shocked, the men whirled to see Vamenos in the door,
wine bottles in each hand.

"A party! Here! Now tell us, who wears the suit first
tonight? Me?"

"It's too late!" said Gómez.

"Late! It's only nine-fifteen!"

"Late?" said everyone, bristling. "Late?"

Gómez edged away from these men who glared from
him to the suit to the open window.

Outside and below it was, after all, thought Martínez,
a fine Saturday night in a summer month and through the
calm warm darkness the women drifted like flowers on a
quiet stream. The men made a mournful sound.

"Gómez, a suggestion." Villanazul licked his pencil
and drew a chart on a pad. "You wear the suit from nine-
thirty to ten, Manulo till ten-thirty, Domínguez till
eleven, myself till eleven-thirty, Martínez till midnight,
and———"

"Why me *last*?" demanded Vamenos, scowling.

Martínez thought quickly and smiled. "After midnight
is the *best* time, friend."

"Hey," said Vamenos, "that's right. I never thought of
that. Okay."

Gómez sighed. "All right. A half hour each. But from
now on, remember, we each wear the suit just one night a
week. Sundays we draw straws for who wears the suit
the extra night."

"Me!" laughed Vamenos. "I'm lucky!"

Gómez held onto Martínez, tight.

"Gómez," urged Martínez, "you first. Dress."

Gómez could not tear his eyes from that disreputable Vamenos. At last, impulsively, he yanked his shirt off over his head. "Ay-yeah!" he howled. *"Ay-yeee!"*

Whisper rustle . . . the clean shirt.

"Ah . . . !"

How clean the new clothes feel, thought Martínez, holding the coat ready. How clean they sound, how clean they smell!

Whisper . . . the pants . . . the tie, rustle . . . the suspenders. Whisper . . . now Martínez let loose the coat, which fell in place on flexing shoulders.

"Ole!"

Gómez turned like a matador in his wonderous suit-of-lights.

"Ole, Gómez, ole!"

Gómez bowed and went out the door.

Martínez fixed his eyes to his watch. At ten sharp he heard someone wandering about in the hall as if they had forgotten where to go. Martínez pulled the door open and looked out.

Gómez was there, heading for nowhere.

He looks sick, thought Martínez. No, stunned, shook up, surprised, many things.

"Gómez! This is the place!"

Gómez turned around and found his way through the door.

"Oh, friends, friends," he said. "Friends, what an experience! This suit! This suit!"

"Tell us, Gómez!" said Martínez.

"I can't, how can I say it!" He gazed at the heavens, arms spread, palms up.

"Tell us, Gómez!"

"I have no words, no words. You must see, yourself! Yes, you must see——" And here he lapsed into silence, shaking his head until at last he remembered they all stood watching him. "Who's next? Manulo?"

Manulo, stripped to his shorts, leapt forward.

"Ready!"

All laughed, shouted, whistled.

Manulo, ready, went out the door. He was gone twenty-nine minutes and thirty seconds. He came back holding to doorknobs, touching the wall, feeling his own elbows, putting the flat of his hand to his face.

"Oh, let me tell you," he said. *"Compadres,* I went to the bar, eh, to have a drink? But no, I did not go in the bar, do you hear? I did not drink. For as I walked I began to laugh and sing. Why, why? I listened to myself and asked this. Because. The suit made me feel better than wine ever did. The suit made me drunk, drunk! So I went to the *Guadalajara Refritería* instead and played the guitar and sang four songs, very high! The suit, ah, the suit!"

Domínguez, next to be dressed, moved out through the world, came back from the world.

The black telephone book! thought Martínez. He had it in his hands when he left! Now, he returns, hands empty! What? What?

"On the street," said Domínguez, seeing it all again, eyes wide, "on the street I walked, a woman cried, 'Dominguez, is that *you?*' Another said, 'Domínguez? No, Quetzalcoatl, the Great White God come from the East,' do you hear? And suddenly I didn't want to go with six women or eight, no. One, I thought. One! And to this one, who knows *what* I would say? 'Be mine!' Or 'Marry me!' *Caramba!* This suit is dangerous! But I did not care! I live, I live! Gómez, did it happen this way with you?"

Gómez, still dazed by the events of the evening, shook his head. "No, no talk. It's too much. Later. Villanazul . . . ?"

Villanazul moved shyly forward.

Villanazul went shyly out.

Villanazul came shyly home.

"Picture it," he said, not looking at them, looking at the floor, talking to the floor. "The Green Plaza, a group of elderly businessmen gathered under the stars and they are talking, nodding, talking. Now one of them whispers. All turn to stare. They move aside, they make a channel through which a white-hot light burns its way as through ice. At the center of the great light is this person. I take

a deep breath. My stomach is jelly. My voice is very
small, but it grows louder. And what do I say? I say,
'Friends. Do you know Carlyle's *Sartor Resartus?* In
that book we find *his* Philosophy of Suits. . . .' "

And at last it was time for Martínez to let the suit
float him out to haunt the darkness.

Four times he walked around the block. Four times
he paused beneath the tenement porches, looking up at
the window where the light was lit; a shadow moved, the
beautiful girl was there, not there, away and gone, and on
the fifth time there she was on the porch above, driven
out by the summer heat, taking the cooler air. She
glanced down. She made a gesture.

At first he thought she was waving to him. He felt
like a white explosion that had riveted her attention.
But she was not waving. Her hand gestured and the
next moment a pair of dark-framed glasses sat upon her
nose. She gazed at him.

Ah, ah, he thought, so that's it. So! Even the blind
may see this suit! He smiled up at her. He did not have
to wave. And at last she smiled back. She did not have
to wave either. Then, because he did not know what else
to do and he could not get rid of this smile that had fas-
tened itself to his cheeks, he hurried, almost ran, around
the corner, feeling her stare after him. When he looked
back she had taken off her glasses and gazed now with
the look of the nearsighted at what, at most, must be a
moving blob of light in the great darkness here. Then
for good measure he went around the block again,
through a city so suddenly beautiful he wanted to yell,
then laugh, then yell again.

Returning, he drifted, oblivious, eyes half closed, and
seeing him in the door, the others saw not Martínez but
themselves come home. In that moment, they sensed
that something had happened to them all.

"You're late!" cried Vamenos, but stopped. The spell
could not be broken.

"Somebody tell me," said Martínez. "Who am I?"

He moved in a slow circle through the room.

Yes, he thought, yes, it's the suit, yes, it had to do
with the suit and them all together in that store on this
fine Saturday night and then here, laughing and feeling

more drunk without drinking as Manulo said himself, as the night ran and each slipped on the pants and held, toppling, to the others and, balanced, let the feeling get bigger and warmer and finer as each man departed and the next took his place in the suit until now here stood Martínez all splendid and white as one who gives orders and the world grows quiet and moves aside.

"Martínez, we borrowed three mirrors while you were gone. Look!"

The mirrors, set up as in the store, angled to reflect three Martínezes and the echoes and memories of those who had occupied this suit with him and known the bright world inside this thread and cloth. Now, in the shimmering mirror, Martínez saw the enormity of this thing they were living together and his eyes grew wet. The others blinked. Martínez touched the mirrors. They shifted. He saw a thousand, a million white-armored Martínezes march off into eternity, reflected, re-reflected, forever, indomitable, and unending.

He held the white coat out on the air. In a trance, the others did not at first recognize the dirty hand that reached to take the coat. Then:

"Vamenos!"

"Pig!"

"You didn't wash!" cried Gómez. "Or even shave, while you waited! *Compadres,* the bath!"

"The bath!" said everyone.

"No!" Vamenos flailed. "The night air! I'm dead!"

They hustled him yelling out and down the hall.

Now here stood Vamenos, unbelievable in white suit, beard shaved, hair combed, nails scrubbed.

His friends scowled darkly at him.

For was it not true, thought Martínez, that when Vamenos passed by, avalanches itched on mountaintops? If he walked under windows, people spat, dumped garbage, or worse. Tonight now, this night, he would stroll beneath ten thousand wide-opened windows, near balconies, past alleys. Suddenly the world absolutely sizzled with flies. And here was Vamenos, a fresh-frosted cake.

"You sure look keen in that suit, Vamenos," said Manulo sadly.

"Thanks." Vamenos twitched, trying to make his skeleton comfortable where all their skeletons had so recently been. In a small voice Vamenos said, "Can I go now?"

"Villanazul!" said Gómez. "Copy down these rules."

Villanazul licked his pencil.

"First," said Gómez, "don't fall down in that suit, Vamenos!"

"I won't."

"Don't lean against buildings in that suit."

"No buildings."

"Don't walk under trees with birds in them in that suit. Don't smoke. Don't drink——"

"Please," said Vamenos, "can I *sit down* in this suit?"

"When in doubt, take the pants off, fold them over a chair."

"Wish me luck," said Vamenos.

"Go with God, Vamenos."

He went out. He shut the door.

There was a ripping sound.

"Vamenos!" cried Martínez.

He whipped the door open.

Vamenos stood with two halves of a handkerchief torn in his hands, laughing.

"Rrrip! Look at your faces! Rrrip!" He tore the cloth again. "Oh, oh, your faces, your faces! Ha!"

Roaring, Vamenos slammed the door, leaving them stunned and alone.

Gómez put both hands on top of his head and turned away. "Stone me. Kill me. I have sold our souls to a demon!"

Villanazul dug in his pockets, took out a silver coin, and studied it for a long while.

"Here is my last fifty cents. Who else will help me buy back Vamenos' share of the suit?"

"It's no use." Manulo showed them ten cents. "We got only enough to buy the lapels and the buttonholes."

Gómez, at the open window, suddenly leaned out and yelled. "Vamenos! No!"

Below on the street, Vamenos, shocked, blew out a match and threw away an old cigar butt he had found somewhere. He made a strange gesture to all the men in the window above, then waved airily and sauntered on.

Somehow, the five men could not move away from the window. They were crushed together there.

"I bet he eats a hamburger in that suit," mused Villanazul. "I'm thinking of the mustard."

"Don't!" cried Gómez. "No, no!"

Manulo was suddenly at the door.

"I need a drink, bad."

"Manulo, there's wine here, that bottle on the floor——"

Manulo went out and shut the door.

A moment later Villanazul stretched with great exaggeration and strolled about the room.

"I think I'll walk down to the plaza, friends."

He was not gone a minute when Domínguez, waving his black book at the others, winked and turned the doorknob.

"Domínguez," said Gómez.

"Yes?"

"If you see Vamenos, by accident," said Gómez, "warn him away from Mickey Murrillo's Red Rooster Café. They got fights not only *on* TV but *out front* of the TV too."

"He wouldn't go into Murrillo's," said Domínguez. "That suit means too much to Vamenos. He wouldn't do anything to hurt it."

"He'd shoot his mother first," said Martínez.

"Sure he would."

Martínez and Gómez, alone, listened to Domínguez's footsteps hurry away down the stairs. They circled the undressed window dummy.

For a long while, biting his lips, Gómez stood at the window, looking out. He touched his shirt pocket twice, pulled his hand away, and then at last pulled something from the pocket. Without looking at it, he handed it to Martínez.

"Martínez, take this."

"What is it?"

Martínez looked at the piece of folded pink paper with print on it, with names and numbers. His eyes widened.

"A ticket on the bus to El Paso three weeks from now!"

Gómez nodded. He couldn't look at Martínez. He stared out into the summer night.

"Turn it in. Get the money," he said. "Buy us a nice white panama hat and a pale blue tie to go with the white ice cream suit, Martínez. Do that."

"Gómez——"

"Shut up. Boy, is it hot in here! I need air."

"Gómez. I am touched. Gómez——"

But the door stood open. Gómez was gone.

Mickey Murrillo's Red Rooster Café and Cocktail Lounge was squashed between two big brick buildings and, being narrow, had to be deep. Outside, serpents of red and sulphur-green neon fizzed and snapped. Inside, dim shapes loomed and swam away to lose themselves in a swarming night sea.

Martínez, on tiptoe, peeked through a flaked place on the red-painted front window.

He felt a presence on his left, heard breathing on his right. He glanced in both directions.

"Manulo! Villanazul!"

"I decided I wasn't thirsty," said Manulo. "So I took a walk."

"I was just on my way to the plaza," said Villanazul, "and decided to go the long way around."

As if by agreement, the three men shut up now and turned together to peer on tiptoe through various flaked spots on the window.

A moment later, all three felt a new very warm presence behind them and heard still faster breathing.

"Is our white suit in there?" asked Gómez's voice.

"Gómez!" said everybody, surprised. "Hi!"

"Yes!" cried Domínguez, having just arrived to find his own peephole. "There's the suit! And, praise God, Vamenos is still *in* it!"

"I can't see!" Gómez squinted, shielding his eyes. "What's he *doing?*"

Martínez peered. Yes! There, way back in the shadows, was a big chunk of snow and the idiot smile of Vamenos winking above it, wreathed in smoke.

"He's smoking!" said Martínez.

"He's drinking!" said Domínguez.

"He's eating a taco!" reported Villanazul.

"A *juicy* taco," added Manulo.

"No," said Gómez. "No, no, no. . . ."

"Ruby Escuadrillo's with him!"

"Let me see that!" Gómez pushed Martínez aside.

Yes, there was Ruby! Two hundred pounds of glittering sequins and tight black satin on the hoof, her scarlet fingernails clutching Vamenos' shoulder. Her cowlike face, floured with powder, greasy with lipstick, hung over him!

"That hippo!" said Domínguez. "She's crushing the shoulder pads. Look, she's going to sit on his lap!"

"No, no, not with all that powder and lipstick!" said Gómez. "Manulo, inside! Grab that drink! Villanazul, the cigar, the taco! Domínguez, date Ruby Escuadrillo, get her away. *Ándale,* men!"

The three vanished, leaving Gómez and Martínez to stare, gasping, through the peephole.

"Manulo, he's got the drink, he's *drinking* it!"

"*Ay!* There's Villanazul, he's got the cigar, he's eating the taco!"

"Hey, Domínguez, he's got Ruby! What a *brave* one!"

A shadow bulked through Murrillo's front door, traveling fast.

"Gómez!" Martínez clutched Gómez's arm. "That was Ruby Escuadrillo's boy friend, Toro Ruíz. If he finds her with Vamenos, the ice cream suit will be covered with blood, *covered* with blood——"

"Don't make me nervous," said Gómez. "Quickly!"

Both ran. Inside they reached Vamenos just as Toro Ruíz grabbed about two feet of the lapels of that wonderful ice cream suit.

"Let go of Vamenos!" said Martínez.

"Let go that *suit!*" corrected Gómez.

Toro Ruíz, tap-dancing Vamenos, leered at these intruders.

Villanazul stepped up shyly.

Villanazul smiled. "Don't hit him. Hit me."

Toro Ruíz hit Villanazul smack on the nose.

Villanazul, holding his nose, tears stinging his eyes, wandered off.

Gómez grabbed one of Toro Ruíz's arms, Martínez the other.

"Drop him, let go, *cabrón, coyote, vaca!*"

Toro Ruíz twisted the ice cream suit material until all six men screamed in mortal agony. Grunting, sweating, Toro Ruíz dislodged as many as climbed on. He was winding up to hit Vamenos when Villanazul wandered back, eyes streaming.

"Don't hit him. Hit me!"

As Toro Ruíz hit Villanazul on the nose, a chair crashed on Toro's head.

"*Ai!*" said Gómez.

Toro Ruíz swayed, blinking, debating whether to fall. He began to drag Vamenos with him.

"Let go!" cried Gómez. "Let go!"

One by one, with great care, Toro Ruíz's banana-like fingers let loose of the suit. A moment later he was ruins at their feet.

"*Compadres,* this way!"

They ran Vamenos outside and set him down where he freed himself of their hands with injured dignity.

"Okay, okay. My time ain't up. I still got two minutes and, let's see—ten seconds."

"What!" said everybody.

"Vamenos," said Gómez, "you let a Guadalajara cow climb on you, you pick fights, you smoke, you drink, you eat tacos, and *now* you have the nerve to say your time ain't up?"

"I got two minutes and one second left!"

"Hey, Vamenos, you sure look sharp!" Distantly, a woman's voice called from across the street.

Vamenos smiled and buttoned the coat.

"It's Ramona Álvarez! Ramona, wait!" Vamenos stepped off the curb.

"Vamenos," pleaded Gómez. "What can you do in one minute and"—he checked his watch—"forty seconds!"

"Watch! Hey, Ramona!"

Vamenos loped.

"Vamenos, look out!"

Vamenos, surprised, whirled, saw a car, heard the shriek of brakes.

"No," said all five men on the sidewalk.

Martínez heard the impact and flinched. His head moved up. It looks like white laundry, he thought, flying through the air. His head came down.

Now he heard himself and each of the men make a different sound. Some swallowed too much air. Some let it out. Some choked. Some groaned. Some cried aloud for justice. Some covered their faces. Martínez felt his own fist pounding his heart in agony. He could not move his feet.

"I don't want to live," said Gómez quietly. "Kill me, someone."

Then, shuffling, Martínez looked down and told his feet to walk, stagger, follow one after the other. He collided with other men. Now they were trying to run. They ran at last and somehow crossed a street like a deep river through which they could only wade, to look down at Vamenos.

"Vamenos!" said Martínez. "You're alive!"

Strewn on his back, mouth open, eyes squeezed tight, tight, Vamenos motioned his head back and forth, back and forth, moaning.

"Tell me, tell me, oh, tell me, tell me."

"Tell you what, Vamenos?"

Vamenos clenched his fists, ground his teeth.

"The suit, what have I done to the suit, the suit, the suit!"

The men crouched lower.

"Vamenos, it's . . . why, it's *okay!*"

"You lie!" said Vamenos. "It's torn, it must be, it must be, it's torn, all around, *underneath?*"

"No." Martínez knelt and touched here and there. "Vamenos, all around, underneath even, it's okay!"

Vamenos opened his eyes to let the tears run free at last. "A miracle," he sobbed. "Praise the saints!" He quieted at last. "The car?"

"Hit and run." Gómez suddenly remembered and glared at the empty street. "It's good he didn't stop. We'd have——"

Everyone listened.

Distantly a siren wailed.

"Someone phoned for an ambulance."

"Quick!" said Vamenos, eyes rolling. "Set me up! Take off our coat!"

"Vamenos——"

"Shut up, idiots!" cried Vamenos. "The coat, that's it! Now, the pants, the pants, quick, quick, *peónes!* Those doctors! You seen movies? They rip the pants with razors to get them off! They don't *care!* They're maniacs! Ah, God, quick, quick!"

The siren screamed.

The men, panicking, all handled Vamenos at once.

"Right leg, *easy,* hurry, cows! Good! Left leg, now, left, you hear, there, easy, *easy!* Ow, God! Quick! Martínez, your pants, take them off!"

"What?" Martínez froze.

The siren shrieked.

"Fool!" wailed Vamenos. "All is lost! Your pants! Give me!"

Martínez jerked at his belt buckle.

"Close in, make a circle!"

Dark pants, light pants flourished on the air.

"Quick, here come the maniacs with the razors! Right leg on, left leg, *there!*"

"The zipper, cows, zip my zipper!" babbled Vamenos.

The siren died.

"Madre mía, yes, just in time! They arrive." Vamenos lay back down and shut his eyes. *"Gracias."*

Martínez turned, nonchalantly buckling on the white pants as the interns brushed past.

"Broken leg," said one intern as they moved Vamenos onto a stretcher.

"Compadres," said Vamenos, "don't be mad with me."

Gómez snorted. "Who's mad?"

In the ambulance, head tilted back, looking out at them upside down, Vamenos faltered.

"Compadres, when . . . when I come from the hospital . . . am I still in the bunch? You won't kick me out? Look, I'll give up smoking, keep away from Murrillo's, swear off women——"

"Vamenos," said Martínez gently, "don't promise nothing."

Vamenos, upside down, eyes brimming wet, saw Martínez there, all white now against the stars.

"Oh, Martínez, you sure look great in that suit. *Compadres,* don't he look *beautiful?*"

Villanazul climbed in beside Vamenos. The door slammed. The four remaining men watched the ambulance drive away.

Then, surrounded by his friends, inside the white suit, Martínez was carefully escorted back to the curb.

In the tenement, Martínez got out the cleaning fluid and the others stood around, telling him how to clean the suit and, later, how not to have the iron too hot and how to work the lapels and the crease and all. When the suit was cleaned and pressed so it looked like a fresh gardenia just opened, they fitted it to the dummy.

"Two o'clock," murmured Villanazul. "I hope Vamenos sleeps well. When I left him at the hospital, he looked good."

Manulo cleared his throat. "Nobody else is going out with that suit tonight, huh?"

The others glared at him.

Manulo flushed. "I mean . . . it's late. We're tired. Maybe no one will use the suit for forty-eight hours, huh? Give it a rest. Sure. Well. Where do we sleep?"

The night being still hot and the room unbearable, they carried the suit on its dummy out and down the hall. They brought with them also some pillows and blankets. They climbed the stairs toward the roof of the tenement. There, thought Martínez, is the cooler wind, and sleep.

On the way, they passed a dozen doors that stood open, people still perspiring and awake, playing cards, drinking pop, fanning themselves with movie magazines.

I wonder, thought Martínez. I wonder if—— Yes!

On the fourth floor, a certain door stood open.

The beautiful girl looked up as the men passed. She wore glasses and when she saw Martínez she snatched them off and hid them under her book.

The others went on, not knowing they had lost Martínez, who seemed stuck fast in the open door.

For a long moment he could say nothing. Then he said: "José Martínez."

And she said:

"Celia Obregón."

And then both said nothing.

He heard the men moving up on the tenement roof. He moved to follow.

She said quickly, "I saw you tonight!"

He came back.

"The suit," he said.

"The suit," she said, and paused. "But not the suit."

"Eh?" he said.

She lifted the book to show the glasses lying in her lap. She touched the glasses.

"I do not see well. You would think I would wear my glasses, but no. I walk around for years now, hiding them, seeing nothing. But tonight, even without the glasses, I see. A great whiteness passes below in the dark. So white! And I put on my glasses quickly!"

"The suit, as I said," said Martínez.

"The suit for a little moment, yes, but there is another whiteness above the suit."

"Another?"

"Your teeth! Oh, such white teeth, and so many!"

Martínez put his hand over his mouth.

"So happy, Mr. Martínez," she said. "I have not often seen such a happy face and such a smile."

"Ah," he said, not able to look at her, his face flushing now.

"So, you see," she said quietly, "the suit caught my eye, yes, the whiteness filled the night below. But the teeth were much whiter. Now, I have forgotten the suit."

Martínez flushed again. She, too, was overcome with what she had said. She put her glasses on her nose, and then took them off, nervously, and hid them again. She looked at her hands and at the door above his head.

"May I——" he said, at last.

"May you——"

"May I call for you," he asked, "when next the suit is mine to wear?"

"Why must you wait for the suit?" she said.

"I thought——"

"You do not need the suit," she said.

"But——"

"If it were just the suit," she said, "anyone would be fine in it. But no, I watched. I saw many men in that suit, all different, this night. So again I say, you do not need to wait for the suit."

"*Madre mía, madre mía!*" he cried happily. And then, quieter, "I will need the suit for a little while. A month, six months, a year. I am uncertain. I am fearful of many things. I am young."

"That is as it should be," she said.

"Good night, Miss——"

"Celia Obregón."

"Celia Obregón," he said, and was gone from the door.

The others were waiting on the roof of the tenement. Coming up through the trapdoor, Martínez saw they had placed the dummy and the suit in the center of the roof and put their blankets and pillows in a circle around it. Now they were lying down. Now a cooler night wind was blowing here, up in the sky.

Martínez stood alone by the white suit, smoothing the lapels, talking half to himself.

"Ay, *caramba*, what a night! Seems ten years since seven o'clock, when it all started and I had no friends. Two in the morning, I got all *kinds* of friends. . . ." He paused and thought, Celia Obregón, Celia Obregón. ". . . all kinds of friends," he went on. "I got a room, I got clothes. You tell *me*. You know what?" He looked around at the men lying on the rooftop, surrounding the dummy and himself. "It's funny. When I wear this suit, I know I will win at pool, like Gómez. A woman will look at me like Domínguez. I will be able to sing like Manulo, sweetly. I will talk fine politics like Villanazul. I'm strong as Vamenos. So? So, tonight, I am more than Martínez. I am Gómez, Manulo, Domínguez, Villanazul, Vamenos. I am everyone. Ay . . . ay . . ." He stood a moment longer by this suit which could save all the ways they sat or stood or walked. This suit which could move fast and nervous like Gómez or slow and thoughtfully like Villanazul or drift like Domínguez, who never touched ground, who always found a wind to take him somewhere. This suit which belonged to them but which also owned them all. This suit that was—what? A parade.

"Martínez," said Gómez. "You going to sleep?"

"Sure. I'm just thinking."

"What?"

"If we ever get rich," said Martínez softly, "it'll be kind of sad. Then we'll all have suits. And there won't be no more nights like tonight. It'll break up the old gang. It'll never be the same after that."

The men lay thinking of what had just been said.

Gómez nodded gently.

"Yeah . . . it'll never be the same . . . after that."

Martínez lay down on his blanket. In darkness, with the others, he faced the middle of the roof and the dummy, which was the center of their lives.

And their eyes were bright, shining, and good to see in the dark as the neon lights from nearby buildings flicked on, flicked off, flicked on, flicked off, revealing and then vanishing, revealing and then vanishing, their wonderful white vanilla ice cream summer suit.

Fever
Dream

They put him between fresh, clean, laundered sheets and there was always a newly squeezed glass of thick orange juice on the table under the dim pink lamp. All Charles had to do was call and Mom or Dad would stick their heads into his room to see how sick he was. The acoustics of the room were fine; you could hear the toilet gargling its porcelain throat of mornings, you could hear rain tap the roof or sly mice run in the secret walls or the canary singing in its cage downstairs. If you were very alert, sickness wasn't too bad.

He was thirteen, Charles was. It was mid-September, with the land beginning to burn with autumn. He lay in the bed for three days before the terror overcame him.

His hand began to change. His right hand. He looked at it and it was hot and sweating there on the counterpane alone. It fluttered, it moved a bit. Then it lay there, changing color.

That afternoon the doctor came again and tapped his thin chest like a little drum. "How are you?" asked the doctor, smiling. "I know, don't tell me: 'My *cold* is fine, Doctor, but *I* feel awful!' Ha!" He laughed at his own oft-repeated joke.

Charles lay there and for him that terrible and ancient

51

jest was becoming a reality. The joke fixed itself in his mind. His mind touched and drew away from it in a pale terror. The doctor did not know how cruel he was with his jokes! "Doctor," whispered Charles, lying flat and colorless. "My *hand,* it doesn't *belong* to me any more. This morning it *changed* into something else. I want you to change it back, Doctor, Doctor!"

The doctor showed his teeth and patted his hand. "It looks fine to me, son. You just had a little fever dream."

"But it changed, Doctor, oh, Doctor," cried Charles, pitifully holding up his pale wild hand. "It *did!*"

The doctor winked. "I'll give you a pink pill for that." He popped a tablet onto Charles' tongue. "Swallow!"

"Will it make my hand change back and become *me,* again?"

"Yes, yes."

The house was silent when the doctor drove off down the road in his car under the quiet, blue September sky. A clock ticked far below in the kitchen world. Charles lay looking at his hand.

It did not change back. It was still something else.

The wind blew outside. Leaves fell against the cool window.

At four o'clock his other hand changed. It seemed almost to become a fever. It pulsed and shifted, cell by cell. It beat like a warm heart. The fingernails turned blue and then red. It took about an hour for it to change and when it was finished, it looked just like any ordinary hand. But it was not ordinary. It no longer was him any more. He lay in a fascinated horror and then fell into an exhausted sleep.

Mother brought the soup up at six. He wouldn't touch it. "I haven't any hands," he said, eyes shut.

"Your hands are perfectly good," said Mother.

"No," he wailed. "My hands are gone. I feel like I have stumps. Oh, Mama, Mama, hold me, hold me, I'm scared!"

She had to feed him herself.

"Mama," he said, "get the doctor, please, again. I'm so sick."

"The doctor'll be here tonight at eight," she said, and went out.

At seven, with night dark and close around the house, Charles was sitting up in bed when he felt the thing happening to first one leg and then the other. "Mama! Come quick!" he screamed.

But when Mama came the thing was no longer happening.

When she went downstairs, he simply lay without fighting as his legs beat and beat, grew warm, red-hot, and the room filled with the warmth of his feverish change. The glow crept up from his toes to his ankles and then to his knees.

"May I come in?" The doctor smiled in the doorway.

"Doctor!" cried Charles. "Hurry, take off my blankets!"

The doctor lifted the blankets tolerantly. "There you are. Whole and healthy. Sweating, though. A little fever. I told you not to move around, bad boy." He pinched the moist pink cheek. "Did the pills help? Did your hand change back?"

"No, no, now it's my other hand and my legs!"

"Well, well, I'll have to give you three more pills, one for each limb, eh, my little peach?" laughed the doctor.

"Will they help me? Please, please. What've I *got?*"

"A mild case of scarlet fever, complicated by a slight cold."

"Is it a germ that lives and has more little germs in me?"

"Yes."

"Are you *sure* it's scarlet fever? You haven't taken any tests!"

"I guess I know a certain fever when I see one," said the doctor, checking the boy's pulse with cool authority.

Charles lay there, not speaking until the doctor was crisply packing his black kit. Then in the silent room, the boy's voice made a small, weak pattern, his eyes alight with remembrance. "I read a book once. About petrified trees, wood turning to stone. About how trees fell and rotted and minerals got in and built up and they look just like trees, but they're not, they're stone." He stopped. In the quiet warm room his breathing sounded.

"Well?" asked the doctor.

"I've been thinking," said Charles after a time. "Do

germs ever get big? I mean, in biology class they told us about one-celled animals, amoebas and things, and how millions of years ago they got together until there was a bunch and they made the first body. And more and more cells got together and got bigger and then finally maybe there was a fish and finally here *we* are, and all we are is a bunch of cells that decided to get together, to help each other out. Isn't that right?" Charles wet his feverish lips.

"What's all this about?" The doctor bent over him.

"I've got to tell you this. Doctor, oh, I've got to!" he cried. "What would happen, oh just pretend, please pretend, that just like in the old days, a lot of microbes got together and wanted to make a bunch, and reproduced and made *more*——"

His white hands were on his chest now, crawling toward his throat.

"And they decided to *take over* a person!" cried Charles.

"Take over a person?"

"Yes, *become* a person. *Me,* my hands, my feet! What if a disease somehow knew how to kill a person and yet live after him?"

He screamed.

The hands were on his neck.

The doctor moved forward, shouting.

At nine o'clock the doctor was escorted out to his car by the mother and father, who handed him his bag. They conversed in the cool night wind for a few minutes. "Just be sure his hands are kept strapped to his legs," said the doctor. "I don't want him hurting himself."

"Will he be all right, Doctor?" The mother held to his arm a moment.

He patted her shoulder. "Haven't I been your family physician for thirty years? It's the fever. He imagines things."

"But those bruises on his throat, he almost choked himself."

"Just you keep him strapped; he'll be all right in the morning."

The car moved off down the dark September road.

At three in the morning, Charles was still awake in his small black room. The bed was damp under his head and his back. He was very warm. Now he no longer had any arms or legs, and his body was beginning to change. He did not move on the bed, but looked at the vast blank ceiling space with insane concentration. For a while he had screamed and thrashed, but now he was weak and hoarse from it, and his mother had gotten up a number of times to soothe his brow with a wet towel. Now he was silent, his hands strapped to his legs.

He felt the walls of his body change, the organs shift, the lungs catch fire like burning bellows of pink alcohol. The room was lighted up as with the flickerings of a hearth.

Now he had no body. It was all gone. It was under him, but it was filled with a vast pulse of some burning, lethargic drug. It was as if a guillotine had neatly lopped off his head, and his head lay shining on a midnight pillow while the body, below, still alive, belonged to somebody else. The disease had eaten his body and from the eating had reproduced itself in feverish duplicate.

There were the little hand hairs and the fingernails and the scars and the toenails and the tiny mole on his right hip, all done again in perfect fashion.

I am dead, he thought. I've been killed, and yet I live. My body is dead, it is all disease and nobody will know. I will walk around and it will not be me, it will be something else. It will be something all bad, all evil, so big and so evil it's hard to understand or think about. Something that will buy shoes and drink water and get married some day maybe and do more evil in the world than has ever been done.

Now the warmth was stealing up his neck, into his cheeks, like a hot wine. His lips burned, his eyelids, like leaves, caught fire. His nostrils breathed out blue flame, faintly, faintly.

This will be all, he thought. It'll take my head and my brain and fix each eye and every tooth and all the marks in my brain, and every hair and every wrinkle in my ears, and there'll be nothing left of me.

He felt his brain fill with a boiling mercury. He felt his left eye clench in upon itself and, like a snail, withdraw, shift. He was blind in his left eye. It no longer belonged to him. It was enemy territory. His tongue was gone, cut out. His left cheek was numbed, lost. His left ear stopped hearing. It belonged to someone else now. This thing that was being born, this mineral thing replacing the wooden log, this disease replacing healthy animal cell.

He tried to scream and he was able to scream loud and high and sharply in the room, just as his brain flooded down, his right eye and right ear were cut out, he was blind and deaf, all fire, all terror, all panic, all death.

His scream stopped before his mother ran through the door to his side.

It was a good, clear morning, with a brisk wind that helped carry the doctor up the path before the house. In the window above, the boy stood, fully dressed. He did not wave when the doctor waved and called, "What's this? Up? My God!"

The doctor almost ran upstairs. He came gasping into the bedroom.

"What are you doing out of bed?" he demanded of the boy. He tapped his thin chest, took his pulse and temperature. "Absolutely amazing! Normal. Normal, by God!"

"I shall never be sick again in my life," declared the boy, quietly, standing there, looking out the wide window. "Never."

"I hope not. Why, you're looking fine, Charles."

"Doctor?"

"Yes, Charles?"

"Can I go to school *now?*" asked Charles.

"Tomorrow will be time enough. You sound positively eager."

"I am. I like school. All the kids. I want to play with them and wrestle with them, and spit on them and play with the girls' pigtails and shake the teacher's hand, and rub my hands on all the cloaks in the cloakroom, and I want to grow up and travel and shake hands with people all over the world, and be married and have lots of children, and go to libraries and handle books and—*all* of that I want to!" said the boy, looking off into the September morning. "What's the name you called me?"

"What?" The doctor puzzled. "I called you nothing but Charles."

"It's better than no name at all, I guess." The boy shrugged.

"I'm glad you want to go back to school," said the doctor.

"I really anticipate it," smiled the boy. "Thank you for your help, Doctor. Shake hands."

"Glad to."

They shook hands gravely, and the clear wind blew through the open window. They shook hands for almost a minute, the boy smiling up at the old man and thanking him.

Then, laughing, the boy raced the doctor downstairs and out to his car. His mother and father followed for the happy farewell.

"Fit as a fiddle!" said the doctor. "Incredible!"

"And strong," said the father. "He got out of his straps himself during the night. Didn't you, Charles?"

"Did I?" said the boy.

"You did! How?"

"Oh," the boy said, "that was a long time ago."

"A long time ago!"

They all laughed, and while they were laughing, the quiet boy moved his bare foot on the sidewalk and merely touched, brushed against a number of red ants that was scurrying about on the sidewalk. Secretly, his eyes shining, while his parents chatted with the old man, he saw the ants hesitate, quiver, and lie still on the cement. He sensed they were cold now.

"Good-by!"

The doctor drove away, waving.

The boy walked ahead of his parents. As he walked he looked away toward the town and began to hum "School Days" under his breath.

"It's good to have him well again," said the father.

"Listen to him. He's so looking forward to school!"

The boy turned quietly. He gave each of his parents a crushing hug. He kissed them both several times.

Then without a word he bounded up the steps into the house.

In the parlor, before the others entered, he quickly opened the bird cage, thrust his hand in, and petted the yellow canary, *once*.

Then he shut the cage door, stood back, and waited.

The
Marriage
Mender

In the sun the headboard was like a fountain, tossing up plumes of clear light. It was carved with lions and gargoyles and bearded goats. It was an awe-inspiring object even at midnight, as Antonio sat on the bed and unlaced his shoes and put his large calloused hand out to touch its shimmering harp. Then he rolled over into this fabulous machine for dreaming, and he lay breathing heavily, his eyes beginning to close.

"Every night," his wife's voice said, "we sleep in the mouth of a calliope."

Her complaint shocked him. He lay a long while before daring to reach up his hard-tipped fingers to stroke the cold metal of the intricate headboard, the threads of this lyre that had sung many wild and beautiful songs down the years.

"This is no calliope," he said.

"It cries like one," Maria said. "A billion people on this world tonight have beds. Why, I ask the saints, not us?"

"This," said Antonio gently, "is a bed." He plucked a little tune on the imitation brass harp behind his head. To his ears it was "Santa Lucia."

"This bed has humps like a herd of camels was under it."

59

"Now, Mama," Antonio said. He called her Mama when she was mad, though they had no children. "You were never this way," he went on, "until five months ago when Mrs. Brancozzi downstairs bought her new bed."

Maria said wistfully, "Mrs. Brancozzi's bed. It's like snow. It's all flat and white and smooth."

"I don't want any damn snow, all flat and white and smooth! These springs—feel them!" he cried angrily. "They know me. They recognize that this hour of night I lie *thus*, at two o'clock, *so!* Three o'clock *this* way, four o'clock *that*. We are like a tumbling act, we've worked together for years and know all the holds and falls."

Maria sighed, and said, "Sometimes I dream we're in the taffy machine at Bartole's candy store."

"This bed," he announced to the darkness, "served our family before Garibaldi! From this wellspring alone came precincts of honest voters, a squad of clean-saluting Army men, two confectioners, a barber, four second leads for *Il Trovatore* and *Rigoletto,* and two geniuses so complex they never *could* decide what to do in their lifetime! Not to forget enough beautiful women to provide ballrooms with their finest decoration. A cornucopia of plenty, this bed! A veritable harvesting machine!"

"We have been married two years," she said with dreadful control over her voice. "Where are *our* second leads for *Rigoletto,* our geniuses, our ballroom decorations?"

"Patience, Mama."

"Don't call me Mama! While this bed is busy favoring you all night, never once has it done for me. Not even so much as a baby *girl!*"

He sat up. "You've let these women in this tenement ruin you with their dollar-down, dollar-a-week talk. Has Mrs. Brancozzi children? Her and her new bed that she's had for five months?"

"No! But *soon!* Mrs. Brancozzi says . . . and her bed, so beautiful."

He slammed himself down and yanked the covers over him. The bed screamed like all the Furies rushing through the night sky, fading away toward the dawn.

The moon changed the shape of the window pattern on

the floor. Antonio awoke. Maria was not beside him.

He got up and went to peer through the half-open door of the bathroom. His wife stood at the mirror looking at her tired face.

"I don't feel well," she said.

"We argued." He put out his hand to pat her. "I'm sorry. We'll think it over. About the bed, I mean. We'll see how the money goes. And if you're not well tomorrow, see the doctor, eh? Now, come back to bed."

At noon the next day, Antonio walked from the lumberyard to a window where stood fine new beds with their covers invitingly turned back.

"I," he whispered to himself, "am a beast."

He checked his watch. Maria, at this time, would be going to the doctor's. She had been like cold milk this morning; he had told her to go. He walked on to the candy-store window and watched the taffy machine folding and threading and pulling. Does taffy scream? he wondered. Perhaps, but so high we cannot hear it. He laughed. Then, in the stretched taffy, he saw Maria. Frowning, he turned and walked back to the furniture store. No. Yes. No. Yes! He pressed his nose to the icy window. Bed, he thought, you in there, new bed, do you *know* me? Will you be kind to my back, nights?"

He took out his wallet slowly, and peered at the money. He sighed, gazed for a long time at that flat marbletop, that unfamiliar enemy, that new bed. Then, shoulders sagging, he walked into the store, his money held loosely in his hand.

"Maria!" He ran up the steps two at a time. It was nine o'clock at night and he had managed to beg off in the middle of his overtime at the lumberyard to rush home. He rushed through the open doorway, smiling.

The apartment was empty.

"Ah," he said disappointedly. He laid the receipt for the new bed on top of the bureau where Maria might see it when she entered. On those few evenings when he worked late she visited with any one of several neighbors downstairs.

I'll go find her, he thought, and stopped. No. I want

to tell her alone. I'll wait. He sat on the bed. "Old bed," he said, "good-by to you. I am very sorry." He patted the brass lions nervously. He paced the floor. *Come on, Maria.* He imagined her smile.

He listened for her quick running on the stair, but he heard only a slow, measured tread. He thought: That's not my Maria, slow like that, no.

The doorknob turned.

"Maria!"

"You're early!" She smiled happily at him. Did she guess? Was it written on his face? "I've been downstairs," she cried, "telling everyone!"

"Telling everyone?"

"The doctor! I saw the doctor!"

"The doctor?" He looked bewildered. "And?"

"And, Papa, *and*——"

"Do you mean—Papa?"

"Papa, Papa, Papa, Papa!"

"Oh," he said, gently, "you walked so carefully on the stairs."

He took hold of her, but not too tight, and he kissed her cheeks, and he shut his eyes, and he yelled. Then he had to wake a few neighbors and tell them, shake them, tell them again. There had to be a little wine and a careful waltz around, an embracing, a trembling, a kissing of brow, eyelids, nose, lips, temples, ears, hair, chin— and then it was past midnight.

"A miracle," he sighed.

They were alone in their room again, the air warm from the people who had been here a minute before, laughing, talking. But now they were alone again.

Turning out the light, he saw the receipt on the bureau. Stunned, he tried to decide in what subtle and delicious way to break this additional news to her.

Maria sat upon her side of the bed in the dark, hypnotized with wonder. She moved her hands as if her body was a strange doll, taken apart, and now to be put back together again, limb by limb, her motions as slow as if she lived beneath a warm sea at midnight. Now, at last, careful not to break herself, she lay back upon the pillow.

"Maria, I have something to tell you."

"Yes?" she said faintly.

"Now that you are as you are." He squeezed her hand. "You deserve the comfort, the rest, the beauty of a new bed."

She did not cry out happily or turn to him or seize him. Her silence was a thinking silence.

He was forced to continue. "This bed is nothing but a pipe organ, a calliope."

"It is a bed," she said.

"A herd of camels sleep under it."

"No," she said quietly, "from it will come precincts of honest voters, captains enough for *three* armies, two ballerinas, a famous lawyer, a very tall policeman, and seven basso profundos, altos, and sopranos."

He squinted across the dimly lighted room at the receipt upon the bureau. He touched the worn mattress under him. The springs moved softly to recognize each limb, each tired muscle, each aching bone.

He sighed. "I never argue with you, little one."

"Mama," she said.

"Mama," he said.

And then as he closed his eyes and drew the covers to his chest and lay in the darkness by the great fountain, in the sight of a jury of fierce metal lions and amber goat and smiling gargoyles, he listened. And he heard it. It was very far away at first, very tentative, but it came clearer as he listened.

Softly, her arm back over her head, Maria's finger tips began to tap a little dance on the gleaming harp strings, on the shimmering brass pipes of the ancient bed. The music was—yes, of course: "Santa Lucia!" His lips moved to it in a warm whisper. Santa Lucia! Santa Lucia.

It was very beautiful.

The
Town
Where
No
One
Got
Off

Crossing the continental United States by night, by day, on the train, you flash past town after wilderness town where nobody ever gets off. Or rather, no person who doesn't *belong,* no person who hasn't roots in these country graveyards ever bothers to visit their lonely stations or attend their lonely views.

I spoke of this to a fellow passenger, another salesman like myself, on the Chicago–Los Angeles train as we crossed Iowa.

"True," he said. "People get off in Chicago; everyone gets off there. People get off in New York, get off in Boston, get off in L.A. People who don't live there go there to see and come back to tell. But what tourist ever just got off at Fox Hill, Nebraska, to *look* at it? You? Me? No! I don't know anyone, got no business there, it's no health resort, so why bother?"

"Wouldn't it be a fascinating change," I said, "some year to plan a really different vacation? Pick some village lost on the plains where you don't know a soul and go there for the hell of it?"

"You'd be bored stiff."

"I'm not bored thinking of it!" I peered out the window. "What's the next town coming up on this line?"

"Rampart Junction."

64

I smiled. "Sounds good. I might get off there."

"You're a liar and a fool. What you want? Adventure? Romance? Go ahead, jump off the train. Ten seconds later you'll call yourself an idiot, grab a taxi, and race us to the next town."

"Maybe."

I watched telephone poles flick by, flick by, flick by. Far ahead I could see the first faint outlines of a town.

"But I don't think so," I heard myself say.

The salesman across from me looked faintly surprised.

For slowly, very slowly, I was rising to stand. I reached for my hat. I saw my hand fumble for my own suitcase. I was surprised myself.

"Hold on!" said the salesman. "What're you doing?"

The train rounded a curve suddenly. I swayed. Far ahead I saw one church spire, a deep forest, a field of summer wheat.

"It looks like I'm getting off the train," I said.

"Sit down," he said.

"No," I said. "There's something about that town up ahead. I've got to go see. I've got the time. I don't have to be in L.A., really, until next Monday. If I don't get off the train now, I'll always wonder what I missed, what I let slip by when I had the chance to see it."

"We were just talking. There's nothing there."

"You're wrong," I said. "There is."

I put my hat on my head and lifted the suitcase in my hand.

"By God," said the salesman, "I think you're really going to do it."

My heart beat quickly. My face was flushed.

The train whistled. The train rushed down the track. The town was near!

"Wish me luck," I said.

"Luck!" he cried.

I ran for the porter, yelling.

There was an ancient flake-painted chair tilted back against the station-platform wall. In this chair, completely relaxed so he sank into his clothes, was a man of some seventy years whose timbers looked as if he'd been nailed there since the station was built. The sun had burned his face dark and tracked his cheek with lizard folds and stitches that held his eyes in a perpetual squint. His hair smoked ash-white in the summer wind. His blue shirt, open at the neck to show white clock springs, was bleached like the staring late afternoon sky. His shoes were blistered as if he had held them, uncaring, in the mouth of a stove, motionless, forever. His shadow under him was stenciled a permanent black.

As I stepped down the old man's eyes flicked every door on the train and stopped, surprised, at me.

I thought he might wave.

But there was only a sudden coloring of his secret eyes; a chemical change that was recognition. Yet he had not twitched so much as his mouth, an eyelid, a finger. An invisible bulk had shifted inside him.

The moving train gave me an excuse to follow it with my eyes. There was no one else on the platform. No autos waited by the cobwebbed, nailed-shut office. I alone had departed the iron thunder to set foot on the choppy waves of platform lumber.

The train whistled over the hill.

Fool! I thought. My fellow passenger had been right. I would panic at the boredom I already sensed in this place. All right, I thought, fool, yes, but run, no!

I walked my suitcase down the platform, not looking at the old man. As I passed, I heard his thin bulk shift again, this time so I could hear it. His feet were coming down to touch and tap the mushy boards.

I kept walking.

"Afternoon," a voice said faintly.

I knew he did not look at me but only at that great cloudless spread of shimmering sky.

"Afternoon," I said.

I started up the dirt road toward the town. One hundred yards away, I glanced back.

The old man, still seated there, stared at the sun, as if posing a question.

I hurried on.

I moved through the dreaming late afternoon town, utterly anonymous and alone, a trout going upstream, not touching the banks of a clear-running river of life that drifted all about me.

My suspicions were confirmed: it was a town where nothing happened, where occurred only the following events:

At four o'clock sharp, the Honneger Hardware door slammed as a dog came out to dust himself in the road. Four-thirty, a straw sucked emptily at the bottom of a soda glass, making a sound like a great cataract in the drugstore silence. Five o'clock, boys and pebbles plunged in the town river. Five-fifteen, ants paraded in the slanting light under some elm trees.

And yet—I turned in a slow circle—somewhere in this town there must be something worth seeing. I knew it was there. I knew I had to keep walking and looking. I knew I would find it.

I walked. I looked.

All through the afternoon there was only one constant and unchanging factor: the old man in the bleached blue pants and shirt was never far away. When I sat in the drugstore he was out front spitting tobacco that rolled itself into tumblebugs in the dust. When I stood by the river he was crouched downstream making a great thing of washing his hands.

Along about seven-thirty in the evening, I was walking for the seventh or eighth time through the quiet streets when I heard footsteps beside me.

I looked over, and the old man was pacing me, looking straight ahead, a piece of dried grass in his stained teeth.

"It's been a long time," he said quietly.

We walked along in the twilight.

"A long time," he said, "waitin' on that station platform."

"You?" I said.

"Me." He nodded in the tree shadows.

"Were you waiting for someone at the station?"

"Yes," he said. "You."

"Me?" The surprise must have shown in my voice. "But why . . . ? You never saw me before in your life."

"Did I say I did? I just said I was waitin'."

We were on the edge of town now. He had turned and I had turned with him along the darkening riverbank toward the trestle where the night trains ran over going east, going west, but stopping rare few times.

"You want to know anything about me?" I asked, suddenly. "You the sheriff?"

"No, not the sheriff. And no, I don't want to know nothing about you." He put his hands in his pockets. The sun was set now. The air was suddenly cool. "I'm just surprised you're here at last, is all."

"Surprised?"

"Surprised," he said, "and . . . pleased."

I stopped abruptly and looked straight at him.

"How long have you been sitting on that station platform?"

"Twenty years, give or take a few."

I knew he was telling the truth; his voice was as easy and quiet as the river.

"Waiting for me?" I said.

"Or someone like you," he said.

We walked on in the growing dark.

"How you like our town?"

"Nice, quiet." I said.

"Nice, quiet." He nodded. "Like the people?"

"People look nice and quiet."

"They are," he said. "Nice, quiet."

I was ready to turn back but the old man kept talking and in order to listen and be polite I had to walk with him in the vaster darkness, the tides of field and meadow beyond town.

"Yes," said the old man, "the day I retired, twenty years ago, I sat down on that station platform and there I been, sittin', doin' nothin', waitin' for something to happen, I didn't know what, I didn't know, I couldn't say. But when it finally happened, I'd know it, I'd look at it and say, yes, sir, that's what I was waitin' for. Train wreck? No. Old woman friend come back to town after fifty years? No. No. It's hard to say. Someone. Something. And it seems to have something to do with you. I wish I could say——"

"Why don't you try?" I said.

The stars were coming out. We walked on.

"Well," he said slowly, "you know much about your own insides?"

"You mean my stomach or you mean psychologically?"

"That's the word. I mean your head, your brain, you know much about *that?*"

The grass whispered under my feet. "A little."

"You hate many people in your time?"

"Some."

"We all do. It's normal enough to hate, ain't it, and not only hate but, while we don't talk about it, don't we sometimes want to hit people who hurt us, even *kill* them?"

"Hardly a week passes we don't get that feeling," I said, "and put it away."

"We put away all our lives," he said. "The town says thus and so, Mom and Dad say this and that, the law says such and such. So you put away one killing and another and two more after that. By the time you're my age, you got lots of that kind of stuff between your ears. And unless you went to war, nothin' ever happened to get rid of it."

"Some men trapshoot or hunt ducks," I said. "Some men box or wrestle."

"And some don't. I'm talkin' about them that don't. Me. All my life I've been saltin' down those bodies, puttin' 'em away on ice in my head. Sometimes you get mad at a town and the people in it for makin' you put things aside like that. You like the old cave men who just gave a hell of a yell and whanged someone on the head with a club."

"Which all leads up to . . . ?"

"Which all leads up to: everybody'd like to do one killin' in his life, to sort of work off that big load of stuff, all those killin's in his mind he never did have the guts to do. And once in a while a man has a chance. Someone runs in front of his car and he forgets the brakes and keeps goin'. Nobody can prove nothin' with that sort of thing. The man don't even tell himself he did it. He just didn't get his foot on the brake in time. But you know and I know what really happened, don't we?"

"Yes," I said.

The town was far away now. We moved over a small stream on a wooden bridge, just near the railway embankment.

"Now," said the old man, looking at the water, "the

only kind of killin' worth doin' is the one where nobody
can guess who did it or why they did it or who they did
it to, right? Well, I got this idea maybe twenty years ago.
I don't think about it every day or every week. Sometimes
months go by, but the idea's this: only one train stops
here each day, sometimes not even that. Now, if you
wanted to kill someone you'd have to wait, wouldn't you,
for years and years, until a complete and actual stranger
came to your town, a stranger who got off the train for no
reason, a man nobody knows and who don't know nobody
in the town. Then, and only then, I thought, sittin' there
on the station chair, you could just go up and when nobody's around, kill him and throw him in the river. He'd
be found miles downstream. Maybe he'd never be found.
Nobody would ever think to come to Rampart Junction
to find him. He wasn't goin' there. He was on his way
someplace else. There, that's my whole idea. And I'd
know that man the minute he got off the train. Know
him, just as clear . . ."

I had stopped walking. It was dark. The moon would
not be up for an hour.

"Would you?" I said.

"Yes," he said. I saw the motion of his head looking at
the stars. "Well, I've talked enough." He sidled close and
touched my elbow. His hand was feverish, as if he had
held it to a stove before touching me. His other hand, his
right hand, was hidden, tight and bunched, in his pocket.
"I've talked enough."

Something screamed.

I jerked my head.

Above, a fast flying night express razored along the
unseen tracks, flourished light on hill, forest, farm, town
dwellings, field, ditch, meadow, plowed earth and water,
then, raving high, cut off away, shrieking, gone. The rails
trembled for a little while after that. Then, silence.

The old man and I stood looking at each other in the
dark. His left hand was still holding my elbow. His other
hand was still hidden.

"May I say something?" I said at last.

The old man nodded.

"About myself," I said. I had to stop. I could hardly
breathe. I forced myself to go on. "It's funny. I've often

thought the same way as you. Sure, just today, going cross-country, I thought, How perfect, how perfect, how really perfect it could be. Business has been bad for me, lately. Wife sick. Good friend died last week. War in the world. Full of boils, myself. It would do me a world of good——"

"What?" the old man said, his hand on my arm.

"To get off this train in a small town," I said, "where nobody knows me, with this gun under my arm, and find someone and kill them and bury them and go back down to the station and get on and go home and nobody the wiser and nobody ever to know who did it, ever. Perfect, I thought, a perfect crime. And I got off the train."

We stood there in the dark for another minute, staring at each other. Perhaps we were listening to each other's hearts beating very fast, very fast indeed.

The world turned under me. I clenched my fists. I wanted to fall. I wanted to scream like the train.

For suddenly I saw that all the things I had just said were not lies put forth to save my life.

All the things I had just said to this man were true.

And now I knew why I had stepped from the train and walked up through this town. I knew what I had been looking for.

I heard the old man breathing hard and fast. His hand was tight on my arm as if he might fall. His teeth were clenched. He leaned toward me as I leaned toward him. There was a terrible silent moment of immense strain as before an explosion.

He forced himself to speak at last. It was the voice of a man crushed by a monstrous burden.

"How do I know you got a gun under your arm?"

"You don't know." My voice was blurred. "You can't be sure."

He waited. I thought he was going to faint.

"That's how it is?" he said.

"That's how it is," I said.

He shut his eyes tight. He shut his mouth tight.

After another five seconds, very slowly, heavily, he managed to take his hand away from my own immensely heavy arm. He looked down at his right hand then, and took it, empty, out of his pocket.

Slowly, with great weight, we turned away from each other and started walking blind, completely blind, in the dark.

The midnight Passenger-to-be-picked-up flare sputtered on the tracks. Only when the train was pulling out of the station did I lean from the open Pullman door and look back.

The old man was seated there with his chair tilted against the station wall, with his faded blue pants and shirt and his sun-baked face and his sun-bleached eyes. He did not glance at me as the train slid past. He was gazing east along the empty rails where tomorrow or the next day or the day after the day after that, a train, some train, any train, might fly by here, might slow, might stop. His face was fixed, his eyes were blindly frozen, toward the east. He looked a hundred years old.

The train wailed.

Suddenly old myself, I leaned out, squinting.

Now the darkness that had brought us together stood between. The old man, the station, the town, the forest, were lost in the night.

For an hour I stood in the roaring blast staring back at all that darkness.

A
Scent
of
Sarsaparilla

Mr. William Finch stood quietly in the dark and blowing attic all morning and afternoon for three days. For three days in late November, he stood alone, feeling the soft white flakes of Time falling out of the infinite cold steel sky, silently, softly, feathering the roof and powdering the eaves. He stood, eyes shut. The attic, wallowed in seas of wind in the long sunless days, creaked every bone and shook down ancient dusts from its beams and warped timbers and lathings. It was a mass of sighs and torments that ached all about him where he stood sniffing its elegant dry perfumes and feeling of its ancient heritages. Ah. Ah.

Listening, downstairs, his wife Cora could not hear him walk or shift or twitch. She imagined she could only hear him breathe, slowly out and in, like a dusty bellows, alone up there in the attic, high in the windy house.

"Ridiculous," she muttered.

When he hurried down for lunch the third afternoon, he smiled at the bleak walls, the chipped plates, the scratched silverware, and even at his wife!

"What's all the excitement?" she demanded.

"Good spirits is all. Wonderful spirits!" he laughed. He seemed almost hysterical with joy. He was seething in a great warm ferment which, obviously, he had trouble concealing. His wife frowned.

"What's that *smell?*"

"Smell, smell, smell?"

"Sarsaparilla." She sniffed suspiciously. "That's what it is!"

"Oh, it couldn't be!" His hysterical happiness stopped as quickly as if she'd switched him off. He seemed stunned, ill at ease, and suddenly very careful.

"Where did you go this morning?" she asked.

"You *know* I was cleaning the attic."

"Mooning over a lot of trash. I didn't hear a sound. Thought maybe you weren't in the attic at all. What's that?" She pointed.

"Well, now how did *those* get there?" he asked the world.

He peered down at the pair of black spring-metal bicycle clips that bound his thin pants cuffs to his bony ankles.

"Found them in the attic," he answered himself. "Remember when we got out on the gravel road in the early morning on our tandem bike, Cora, forty years ago, everything fresh and new?"

"If you don't finish that attic today, I'll come up and toss everything out myself."

"Oh, no," he cried. "I have everything the way I want it!"

She looked at him coldly.

"Cora," he said, eating his lunch, relaxing, beginning to enthuse again, "you know what attics are? They're Time Machines, in which old, dim-witted men like me can travel back forty years to a time when it was summer all year round and children raided ice wagons. Remember how it tasted? You held the ice in your handkerchief. It was like sucking the flavor of linen and snow at the same time."

Cora fidgeted.

It's not impossible, he thought, half closing his eyes, trying to see it and build it. Consider an attic. Its very atmosphere is Time. It deals in other years, the cocoons and chrysalises of another age. All the bureau drawers are little coffins where a thousand yesterdays lie in state. Oh, the attic's a dark, friendly place, full of Time, and if you stand in the very center of it, straight and tall, squinting your eyes, and thinking and thinking, and smelling the Past, and putting out your hands to feel of Long Ago, why, it . . .

He stopped, realizing he had spoken some of this aloud. Cora was eating rapidly.

"Well, wouldn't it be interesting," he asked the part in her hair, "if Time Travel *could* occur? And what more logical, proper place for it to happen than in an attic like *ours,* eh?"

"It's not always summer back in the old days," she said. "It's just your crazy memory. You remember all the good things and forget the bad. It wasn't always summer."

"Figuratively speaking, Cora, it was."

"Wasn't."

"What I mean is this," he said, whispering excitedly, bending forward to see the image he was tracing on the blank dining-room wall. "If you rode your unicycle carefully between the years, balancing, hands out, careful, careful, if you rode from year to year, spent a week in 1909, a day in 1900, a month or a fortnight somewhere else, 1905, 1898, you could stay with summer the rest of your life."

"Unicycle?"

"You know, one of those tall chromium one-wheeled bikes, single-seater, the performers ride in vaudeville shows, juggling. Balance, true balance, it takes, not to fall off, to keep the bright objects flying in the air, beautiful, up and up, a light, a flash, a sparkle, a bomb of brilliant colors, red, yellow, blue, green, white, gold; all the Junes and Julys and Augusts that ever were, in the air, about you, at once, hardly touching your hands, flying, suspended, and you, smiling, among them. Balance, Cora, *balance*."

"Blah," she said, "blah, blah." And added, "blah!"

He climbed the long cold stairs to the attic, shivering.

There were nights in winter when he woke with porcelain in his bones, with cool chimes blowing in his ears, with frost piercing his nerves in a raw illumination like white-cold fireworks exploding and showering down in flaming snows upon a silent land deep in his subconscious. He was cold, cold, cold, and it would take a score of endless summers, with their green torches and bronze suns to thaw him free of his wintry sheath. He was a great tasteless chunk of brittle ice, a snowman put to bed each night, full of confetti dreams, tumbles of crystal and flurry. And there lay winter outside forever, a great leaden wine press smashing down its colorless lid of sky, squashing them all like so many grapes, mashing color and sense and being from everyone, save the children who fled on skis and toboggans down mirrored hills which re-flected the crushing iron shield that hung lower above town each day and every eternal night.

Mr. Finch lifted the attic trap door. But here, *here*. A dust of summer sprang up about him. The attic dust sim-mered with heat left over from other seasons. Quietly, he shut the trap door down.

He began to smile.

The attic was quiet as a thundercloud before a storm. On occasion, Cora Finch heard her husband murmuring, murmuring, high up there.

At five in the afternoon, singing *My Isle of Golden Dreams*, Mr. Finch flipped a crisp new straw hat in the kitchen door. "Boo!"

"Did you sleep all afternoon?" snapped his wife. "I called up at you four times and no answer."

"Sleep?" He considered this and laughed, then put his hand quickly over his mouth. "Well, I guess I did."

Suddenly she saw him. "My God!" she cried, "where'd you get that coat?"

He wore a red candy-striped coat, a high white, choking collar and ice cream pants. You could smell the straw hat like a handful of fresh hay fanned in the air.

"Found 'em in an old trunk."

She sniffed. "Don't smell of moth balls. Looks brand-new."

"Oh, no!" he said hastily. He looked stiff and uncom-fortable as she eyed his costume.

"This isn't a summer-stock company," she said.

"Can't a fellow have a little fun?"

"That's all you've ever had," she slammed the oven door. "While I've stayed home and knitted, lord knows, you've been down at the store helping ladies' elbows in and out doors."

He refused to be bothered. "Cora." He looked deep into the crackling straw hat. "Wouldn't it be nice to take a Sunday walk the way we used to do, with your silk parasol and your long dress whishing along, and sit on those wire-legged chairs at the soda parlor and smell the drugstore the way they used to smell? Why don't drugstores smell that way any more? And order two sarsaparillas for us, Cora, and then ride out in our 1910 Ford to Hannahan's Pier for a box supper and listen to the brass band. How about it?"

"Supper's ready. Take that dreadful uniform off."

"If you could make a wish and take a ride on those oak-laned country roads like they had before cars started rushing, would you *do* it?" he insisted, watching her.

"Those old roads were dirty. We came home looking like Africans. Anyway," she picked up a sugar jar and shook it, "this morning I had forty dollars here. Now it's gone! Don't tell me you ordered those clothes from a costume house. They're brand-new; they didn't come from any trunk!"

"I'm——" he said.

She raved for half an hour, but he could not bring himself to say anything. The November wind shook the house and as she talked, the snows of winter began to fall again in the cold steel sky.

"Answer me!" she cried. "Are you crazy, spending our money that way, on clothes you can't wear?"

"The attic," he started to say.

She walked off and sat in the living room.

The snow was falling fast now and it was a cold dark November evening. She heard him climb up the stepladder, slowly, into the attic, into that dusty place of other years, into that black place of costumes and props and Time, into a world separate from this world below.

He closed the trap door down. The flashlight, snapped on, was company enough. Yes, here was all of Time compressed in a Japanese paper flower. At the touch of memory, everything would unfold into the clear water of the

mind, in beautiful blooms, in spring breezes, larger than
life. Each of the bureau drawers slid forth, might contain
aunts and cousins and grandmamas, ermined in dust.
Yes, Time was here. You could feel it breathing, an
atmospheric instead of a mechanical clock.

Now the house below was as remote as another day in
the past. He half shut his eyes and looked and looked on
every side of the waiting attic.

Here, in prismed chandelier, were rainbows and mornings and noons as bright as new rivers flowing endlessly
back through time. His flashlight caught and flickered them
alive, the rainbows leapt up to curve the shadows back
with colors, with colors like plums and strawberries and
Concord grapes, with colors like cut lemons and the sky
where the clouds drew off after storming and the blue
was there. And the dust of the attic was incense burning
and all of time burning, and all you need do was peer into
the flames. It was indeed a great machine of Time, this
attic, he knew, he felt, he was sure, and if you touched
prisms here, doorknobs there, plucked tassels, chimed
crystals, swirled dust, punched trunk hasps and gusted
the vox humana of the old hearth bellows until it puffed
the soot of a thousand ancient fires into your eyes, if,
indeed, you played this instrument, this warm machine of
parts, if you fondled all of its bits and pieces, its levers
and changers and movers, then, then, *then!*

He thrust out his hands to orchestrate, to conduct, to
flourish. There was music in his head, in his mouth shut
tight, and he played the great machine, the thunderously
silent organ, bass, tenor, soprano, low, high, and at last,
at last, a chord that shuddered him so that he had to shut
his eyes.

About nine o'clock that night she heard him calling,
"Cora!" She went upstairs. His head peered down at her
from above, smiling at her. He waved his hat. "Good-by,
Cora."

"What do you mean?" she cried.

"I've thought it over for three days and I'm saying
good-by."

"Come down out of there, you fool!"

"I drew five hundred dollars from the bank yesterday.
I've been thinking about this. And then when *it* hap-

pened, well . . . Cora . . ." He shoved his eager hand down. "For the last time, will you come along with me?"

"In the attic? Hand down that stepladder, William Finch. I'll climb up there and run you out of that filthy place!"

"I'm going to Hannahan's Pier for a bowl of clam chowder," he said. "And I'm requesting the brass band to play 'Moonlight Bay.' Oh, come on, Cora . . ." He motioned his extended hand.

She simply stared at his gentle, questioning face.

"Good-by," he said.

He waved gently, gently. Then his face was gone, the straw hat was gone.

"William!" she screamed.

The attic was dark and silent.

Shrieking, she ran and got a chair and used it to groan her way up into the musty darkness. She flourished a flashlight. "William! William!"

The dark spaces were empty. A winter wind shook the house.

Then she saw the far west attic window, ajar.

She fumbled over to it. She hesitated, held her breath. Then, slowly, she opened it. The ladder was placed outside the window, leading down onto a porch roof.

She pulled back from the window.

Outside the opened frame the apple trees shone bright green, it was twilight of a summer day in July. Faintly, she heard explosions, firecrackers going off. She heard laughter and distant voices. Rockets burst in the warm air, softly, red, white, and blue, fading.

She slammed the window and stood reeling. "William!"

Wintry November light glowed up through the trap in the attic floor behind her. Bent to it, she saw the snow whispering against the cold clear panes down in that November world where she would spend the next thirty years.

She did not go near the window again. She sat alone in the black attic, smelling the one smell that did not seem to fade. It lingered like a sigh of satisfaction, on the air. She took a deep, long breath.

The old, the familiar, the unforgettable scent of drugstore sarsaparilla.

Icarus
Montgolfier
Wright

He lay on his bed and the wind blew through the window over his ears and over his half-opened mouth so it whispered to him in his dream. It was like the wind of time hollowing the Delphic caves to say what must be said of yesterday, today, tomorrow. Sometimes one voice gave a shout far off away, sometimes two, a dozen, an entire race of men cried out through his mouth, but their words were always the same:

"Look, look, we've done it!"

For suddenly he, they, one or many, were flung in the dream, and flew. The air spread in a soft warm sea where he swam, disbelieving.

"Look, look! It's done!"

But he didn't ask the world to watch; he was only shocking his senses wide to see, taste, smell, touch the air, the wind, the rising moon. He swam alone in the sky. The heavy earth was gone.

But wait, he thought, wait now!

Tonight—what night is this?

The night before, of course. The night before the first flight of a rocket to the Moon. Beyond this room on the baked desert floor one hundred yards away the rocket waits for me.

Well, does it now? Is there *really* a rocket?

Hold on! he thought, and twisted, turned, sweating, eyes tight, to the wall, the fierce whisper in his teeth. Be certain-sure! You, now, who *are* you?

Me? he thought. *My* name?

Jedediah Prentiss, born 1938, college graduate 1959, licensed rocket pilot, 1965. Jedediah Prentiss . . . Jedediah Prentiss. . . .

The wind whistled his name away! He grabbed for it, yelling.

Then, gone quiet, he waited for the wind to bring his name back. He waited a long while, and there was only silence, and then after a thousand heartbeats he felt motion.

The sky opened out like a soft blue flower. The Aegean Sea stirred soft white fans through a distant wine-colored surf.

In the wash of the waves on the shore, he heard his name.

Icarus.

And again in a breathing whisper.

Icarus.

Someone shook his arm and it was his father saying his name and shaking away the night. And he himself lay small, half-turned to the window and the shore below and the deep sky, feeling the first wind of morning ruffle the golden feathers bedded in amber wax lying by the side of his cot. Golden wings stirred half-alive in his father's arms, and the faint down on his own shoulders quilled trembling as he looked at these wings and beyond them to the cliff.

"Father, how's the wind?"

"Enough for me, but never enough for you. . . ."

"Father, don't worry. The wings seem clumsy now, but my bones in the feathers will make them strong, my blood in the wax will make it live!"

"My blood, my bones too, remember; each man lends his flesh to his children, asking that they tend it well. Promise you'll not go high, Icarus. *The* sun or *my* son, the heat of one, the fever of the other, could melt these wings. Take care!"

And they carried the splendid golden wings into the morning and heard them whisper in their arms, whisper his name or a name or some name that blew, spun, and settled like a feather on the soft air.

Montgolfier.

His hands touched fiery rope, bright linen, stitched thread gone hot as summer. His hands fed wool and straw to a breathing flame.

Montgolfier.

And his eye soared up along the swell and sway, the oceanic tug and pull, the immensely wafted silver pear still filling with the shimmering tidal airs channeled up from the blaze. Silent as a god tilted slumbering above French countryside, this delicate linen envelope, this swelling sack of oven-baked air would soon pluck itself free. Draughting upward to blue worlds of silence, his mind and his brother's mind would sail with it, muted, serene among island clouds where uncivilized lightnings slept. Into that uncharted gulf and abyss where no bird-song or shout of man could follow, the balloon would hush itself. So cast adrift, he, Montgolfier, and all men, might hear the unmeasured breathing of God and the cathedral tread of eternity.

"Ah . . ." He moved, the crowd moved, shadowed by the warm balloon. "Everything's ready, everything's right. . . ."

Right. His lips twitched in his dream. Right. Hiss, whisper, flutter, rush. Right.

From his father's hands a toy jumped to the ceiling, whirled in its own wind, suspended, while he and his brother stared to see it flicker, rustle, whistle, heard it murmuring their names.

Wright.

Whispering: wind, sky, cloud, space, wing, fly . . .

"Wilbur, Orville? Look, how's *that?*"

Ah. In his sleep, his mouth sighed.

The toy helicopter hummed, bumped the ceiling, murmured eagle, raven, sparrow, robin, hawk; murmured eagle, raven, sparrow, robin, hawk. Whispered eagle, whispered raven, and at last, fluttering to their hands with a susurration, a wash of blowing weather from summers yet to come, with a last whir and exhalation, whispered hawk.

Dreaming, he smiled.

He saw the clouds rush down the Aegean sky.

He felt the balloon sway drunkenly, its great bulk ready for the clear running wind.

He felt the sand hiss up the Atlantic shelves from the soft dunes that might save him if he, a fledgling bird, should fall. The framework struts hummed and chorded like a harp, and himself caught up in its music.

Beyond this room he felt the primed rocket glide on the desert field, its fire-wings folded, its fire-breath kept, held ready to speak for three billion men. In a moment he would wake and walk slowly out to that rocket.

And stand on the rim of the cliff.

Stand cool in the shadow of the warm balloon.

Stand whipped by tidal sands drummed over Kitty Hawk.

And sheathe his boy's wrists, arms, hands, fingers with golden wings in golden wax.

And touch for a final time the captured breath of man, the warm gasp of awe and wonder siphoned and sewn to lift their dreams.

And spark the gasoline engine.

And take his father's hand and wish him well with his own wings, flexed and ready, here on the precipice.

Then whirl and jump.

Then cut the cords to free the great balloon.

Then rev the motor, prop the plane on air.

And crack the switch, to fire the rocket fuse.

And together in a single leap, swim, rush, flail, jump, sail, and glide, upturned to sun, moon, stars, they would go above Atlantic, Mediterranean; over country, wilderness, city, town; in gaseous silence, riffling feather, rattle-drum frame, in volcanic eruption, in timid, sputtering roar; in start, jar, hesitation, then steady ascension, beautifully held, wondrously transported, they would laugh and cry each his own name to himself. Or shout the names of others unborn or others long-dead and blown away by the wine wind or the salt wind or the silent hush of balloon wind or the wind of chemical fire. Each feeling the bright feathers stir and bud deep-buried and thrusting to burst from their riven shoulder blades! Each leaving behind the echo of their flying, a sound to encircle, recircle the earth in the winds and speak again in other years to the sons of the sons of their sons, asleep but hearing the restless midnight sky.

Up, yet further up, higher, higher! A spring tide, a summer flood, an unending river of wings!

A bell rang softly.

No, he whispered, I'll wake in a moment. Wait . . .

The Aegean slid away below the window, gone; the Atlantic dunes, the French countryside, dissolved down to New Mexico desert. In his room near his cot stirred no plumes in golden wax. Outside, no wind-sculpted pear, no trap-drum butterfly machine. Outside only a rocket, a combustible dream, waiting for the friction of his hand to set it off.

In the last moment of sleep someone asked his name.

Quietly, he gave the answer as he had heard it during the hours from midnight on.

"Icarus Montgolfier Wright."

He repeated it slowly so the questioner might remember the order and spelling down to the last incredible letter.

"Icarus Montgolfier Wright.

"Born: nine hundred years before Christ. Grammar school: Paris, 1783. High school, college: Kitty Hawk, 1903. Graduation from Earth to Moon: this day, God willing, August 1, 1970. Death and burial, with luck, on Mars, summer 1999 in the Year of Our Lord."

Then he let himself drift awake.

Moments later, crossing the desert Tarmac, he heard someone shouting again and again and again.

And if no one was there or if someone was there behind him, he could not tell. And whether it was one voice or many, young or old, near or very far away, rising or falling, whispering or shouting to him all three of his brave new names, he could not tell, either. He did not turn to see.

For the wind was slowly rising and he let it take hold and blow him all the rest of the way across the desert to the rocket which stood waiting there.

The
Headpiece

The parcel arrived in the late afternoon mail. Mr. Andrew Lemon knew what was inside by shaking it. It whispered in there like a large hairy tarantula.

It took him some time to get up his courage, tremble the wrappings open, and remove the lid from the white cardboard box.

There the bristly thing lay on its snowy tissue bed, as impersonal as the black horsehair clock springs stuffed in an old sofa. Andrew Lemon chuckled.

"Indians come and gone, left this piece of a massacre behind as a sign, a warning. Well. *There!*"

And he fitted the new patent-leather black shining toupee to his naked scalp. He tugged at it like someone touching his cap to passers-by.

The toupee fit perfectly, covering the neat coin-round hole which marred the top of his brow. Andrew Lemon gazed at the strange man in the mirror and yelled with delight.

"Hey there, who're you? Face's familiar, but, by gosh now, pass you on the street without looking twice! Why? Because, *it's* gone! Darn hole's covered, nobody'd guess it was ever there. Happy New Year, man, that's what it is, Happy New Year!"

He walked around and around his little apartment, smil-

ing, needing to do something, but not yet ready to open
the door and surprise the world. He walked by the mirror, glancing sidewise at someone going past there and
each time laughed and shook his head. Then he sat down
in the rocker and rocked, grinning, and tried to look at a
couple of copies of *Wild West Weekly* and then *Thrilling
Movie Magazine*. But he couldn't keep his right hand from
crawling up along his face, tremulously, to feel at the rim
of that crisp new sedge above his ears.

"Let me buy you a drink, young fellow!"

He opened the fly-specked medicine cabinet and took
three gulps from a bottle. Eyes watering, he was on the
verge of cutting himself a chew of tobacco when he
stopped, listening.

Outside in the dark hallway there was a sound like a
field mouse moving softly, daintily on the threadbare carpeting.

"Miss Fremwell!" he said to the mirror.

Suddenly the toupee was off his head and into the box
as if, frightened, it had scuttled back there of itself. He
clapped the lid down, sweating cold, afraid of even the
sound that woman made moving by like a summer breeze.

He tiptoed to a door that was nailed shut in one wall
and bent his raw and now furiously blushing head. He
heard Miss Fremwell unlock her door and shut it and
move delicately about her room with little tinkles of china-
ware and chimes of cutlery, turning in a merry-go-round
to make her dinner. He backed away from that door that
was bolted, locked, latched, and driven shut with its four-
inch hard steel nails. He thought of the nights he had
flinched in bed, thinking he heard her quietly pulling out
the nails, pulling out the nails, touching at the bolts and
slithering the latch . . . And how it always took him an
hour to turn away toward sleep after that.

Now she would rustle about her room for an hour or
so. It would grow dark. The stars would be out and shining when he tapped on her door and asked if she'd sit on
the porch or walk in the park. Then the only way she
could possibly know of this third blind and staring eye in
his head would be to run her hand in a Braille-like motion
there. But her small white fingers had never moved within

a thousand miles of that scar which was no more to her than, well, one of those pockmarks off on the full moon tonight. His toe brushed a copy of *Wonder Science Tales*. He snorted. Perhaps if she thought at all of his damaged head—she wrote songs and poems, didn't she, once in a while?—she figured that a long time back a meteor had run and hit him and vanished up there where there were no shrubs or trees, where it was just white, above his eyes. He snorted again and shook his head. Perhaps, perhaps. But however she thought, he would see her only when the sun had set.

He waited another hour, from time to time spitting out the window into the warm summer night.

"Eight-thirty. Here goes."

He opened the hall door and stood for a moment looking back at that nice new toupee hidden in its box. No, he still could not bring himself to wear it.

He stepped along the hall to Miss Naomi Fremwell's door, a door so thinly made it seemed to beat with the sound of her small heart there behind it.

"Miss Fremwell," he whispered.

He wanted to cup her like a small white bird in his great bowled hands, speak soft to her quietness. But then, in wiping the sudden perspiration from his brow, he found again the pit and only at the last quick moment saved himself from falling over, in, and screaming, down! He clapped his hand to that place to cover that emptiness. After he had held his hand tight to the hole for a long moment he was then afraid to pull his hand away. It had changed. Instead of being afraid he might fall in there, he was afraid something terrible, something secret, something private, might gush out and drown him.

He brushed his free hand across her door, disturbing little more than dust.

"Miss Fremwell?"

He looked to see if there were too many lamps lit under her doorsill, the light of which might strike out at him when she swung the door wide. The very thrust of lamplight alone might knock his hand away, and reveal that sunken wound. Then mightn't she peer through it, like a keyhole, into his life?

The light was dim under the doorsill.

He made a fist of one hand and brought it down gently, three times, on Miss Fremwell's door.

The door opened and moved slowly back.

Later, on the front porch, feverishly adjusting and re-adjusting his senseless legs, perspiring, he tried to work around to asking her to marry him. When the moon rose high, the hole in his brow looked like a leaf shadow fallen there. If he kept one profile to her, the crater did not show; it was hidden away over on the other side of his world. It seemed that when he did this, though, he only had half as many words and felt only half a man.

"Miss Fremwell," he managed to say at last.

"Yes?" She looked at him as if she didn't quite see him.

"Miss Naomi, I don't suppose you ever really noticed me lately."

She waited. He went on.

"I've been noticing you. Fact is, well, I might as well put it right out on the line and get it over with. We been sitting out here on the porch for quite a few months. I mean we've known each other a long time. Sure, you're a good fifteen years younger than me, but would there be anything wrong with our getting engaged, do you think?"

"Thank you very much, Mr. Lemon," she said quickly. She was very polite. "But I——"

"Oh, I know," he said, edging forward with the words. "I know! It's my head, it's always this darn thing up here on my head!"

She looked at his turned-away profile in the uncertain light.

"Why, no, Mr. Lemon, I don't think I would say that, I don't think that's it at all. I have wondered a bit about it, certainly, but I don't think it's an interference in any way. A friend of mine, a very dear friend, married a man once, I recall, who had a wooden leg. She told me she didn't even know he had it after a while."

"It's always this darn hole," cried Mr. Lemon bitterly. He took out his plug of tobacco, looked at it as if he might bite it, decided not to, and put it away. He formed a couple of fists and stared at them bleakly as if they were big rocks. "Well, I'll tell you all about it, Miss Naomi. I'll tell you how it happened."

"You don't have to if you don't want."

"I was married once, Miss Naomi. Yes, I was, darn it. And one day my wife she just took hold of a hammer and hit me right on the head!"

Miss Fremwell gasped. It was as if she had been struck herself.

Mr. Lemon brought one clenching fist down through the warm air.

"Yes, ma'am, she hit me straight on with that hammer, she did. I tell you, the world blew up on me. Everything fell down on me. It was like the house coming down in one heap. That one little hammer buried me, *buried* me! The pain? I can't tell you!"

Miss Fremwell turned in on herself. She shut her eyes and thought, biting her lips. Then she said, "Oh, poor Mr. Lemon."

"She did it so calm," said Mr. Lemon, puzzled. "She just stood over me where I lay on the couch and it was a Tuesday afternoon about two o'clock and she said, 'Andrew, wake up!' and I opened my eyes and looked at her is all and then she hit me with that hammer. Oh, Lord."

"But why?" asked Miss Fremwell.

"For no reason, no reason at all. Oh, what an ornery woman."

"But why should she do a thing like that?" said Miss Fremwell.

"I told you: for no reason."

"Was she crazy?"

"Must of been. Oh, yes, she *must* of been."

"Did you prosecute her?"

"Well, no, I didn't. After all, she didn't know what she was doing."

"Did it knock you out?"

Mr. Lemon paused and there it was again, so clear, so tall, in his mind, the old thought of it. Seeing it there, he put it in words.

"No, I remember just standing up. I stood up and I said to her, 'What'd you do?' and I stumbled toward her. There was a mirror. I saw the hole in my head, deep, and blood coming out. It made an Indian of me. She just stood there, my wife did. And at last she screamed three kinds of horror and dropped that hammer on the floor and ran out the door."

"Did you faint then?"

"No. I didn't faint. I got out on the street some way and I mumbled to somebody I needed a doctor. I got on a bus, mind you, a bus! And paid my fare! And said to leave me by some doctor's house downtown. Everybody screamed, I tell you. I got sort of weak then, and next thing I knew the doctor was working on my head, had it cleaned out like a new thimble, like a bunghole in a barrel. . . ."

He reached up and touched that spot now, fingers hovering over it as a delicate tongue hovers over the vacated area where once grew a fine tooth.

"A neat job. The doctor kept staring at me too, as if he expected me to fall down dead any minute."

"How long did you stay in the hospital?"

"Two days. Then I was up and around, feeling no better, no worse. By that time my wife had picked up and skedaddled."

"Oh, my goodness, my goodness," said Miss Fremwell, recovering her breath. "My heart's going like an egg beater. I can hear and feel and see it all, Mr. Lemon. Why, why, oh, *why* did she do it?"

"I already told you, for no reason I could see. She was just took with a notion, I guess."

"But there must have been an argument——?"

Blood drummed in Mr. Lemon's cheeks. He felt that place up there on his head glow like a fiery crater. "There wasn't no argument. I was just sitting, peaceful as you please. I like to sit, my shoes off, my shirt unbuttoned, afternoons."

"Did you—did you know any other women?"

"No, never, none!"

"You didn't—drink?"

"Just a nip once in a while, you know how it is."

"Did you gamble?"

"No, no, no!"

"But a hole punched in your head like that, Mr. Lemon, my land, my land! All over nothing?"

"You women are all alike. You see something and right off you expect the worst. I tell you there was no reason. She just fancied hammers."

"What did she say before she hit you?"

"Just 'Wake up, Andrew.' "

"No, before that."

"Nothing. Not for half an hour or an hour, anyway. Oh, she said something about wanting to go shopping for something or other, but I said it was too hot. I'd better lie down, I didn't feel so good. She didn't appreciate how I felt. She must have got mad and thought about it for an hour and grabbed that hammer and come in and gone kersmash. I think the weather got her too."

Miss Fremwell sat back thoughtfully in the lattice shadow, her brows moving slowly up and then slowly down.

"How long were you married to her?"

"A year. I remember we got married in July and in July it was I got sick."

"Sick?"

"I wasn't a well man. I worked in a garage. Then I got these backaches so I couldn't work and had to lie down afternoons. Ellie, she worked in the First National Bank."

"I see," said Miss Fremwell.

"What?"

"Nothing," she said.

"I'm an easy man to get on with. I don't talk too much. I'm easygoing and relaxed. I don't waste money. I'm economical. Even Ellie had to admit that. I don't argue. Why, sometimes Ellie would jaw at me and jaw at me, like bouncing a ball hard on a house, but me not bouncing back. I just sat. I took it easy. What's the use of always stirring around and talking, right?"

Miss Fremwell looked over at Mr. Lemon's brow in the moonlight. Her lips moved, but he could not hear what she said.

Suddenly she straightened up and took a deep breath and blinked around surprised to see the world out beyond the porch lattice. The sounds of traffic came in to the porch now, as if they had been tuned up; they had been so quiet for a time. Miss Fremwell took a deep breath and let it out.

"As you yourself say, Mr. Lemon, nobody ever got anywhere arguing."

"Right!" he said. "I'm easygoing, I tell you——"

But Miss Fremwell's eyes were lidded now and her mouth was strange. He sensed this and tapered off.

A night wind blew fluttering her light summer drress and the sleeves of his shirt.

"It's late," said Miss Fremwell.

"Only nine o'clock!"

"I have to get up early tomorrow."

"But you haven't answered my question yet, Miss Fremwell."

"Question?" She blinked. "Oh, the question. Yes." She rose from the wicker seat. She hunted around in the dark for the screen-door knob. "Oh now, Mr. Lemon, let me think it over."

"That's fair enough," he said. "No use arguing, is there?"

The screen door closed. He heard her find her way down the dark warm hall. He breathed shallowly, feeling of the third eye in his head, the eye that saw nothing.

He felt a vague unhappiness shift around inside his chest like an illness brought on by too much talking. And then he thought of the fresh white gift box waiting with its lid on in his room. He quickened. Opening the screen door, he walked down the silent hall and went into his room. Inside he slipped and almost fell on a slick copy of *True Romance Tales*. He switched on the light excitedly, smiling, fumbled the box open, and lifted the toupee from the tissues. He stood before the bright mirror and followed directions with the spirit gum and tapes and tucked it here and stuck it there and shifted it again and combed it neat. Then he opened the door and walked along the hall to knock for Miss Fremwell.

"Miss Naomi?" he called, smiling.

The light under her door clicked out at the sound of his voice.

He stared at the dark keyhole with disbelief.

"Oh, Miss Naomi?" he said again, quickly.

Nothing happened in the room. It was dark. After a moment he tried the knob experimentally. The knob rattled. He heard Miss Fremwell sigh. He heard her say something. Again the words were lost. Her small feet tapped to the door. The light came on.

"Yes?" she said, behind the panel.

"Look, Miss Naomi," he entreated. "Open the door. Look."

The bolt of the door snapped back. She jerked the door open about an inch. One of her eyes looked at him sharply.

"Look," he announced proudly, adjusting the toupee so it very definitely covered the sunken crater. He imagined he saw himself in her bureau mirror and was pleased. "Look here, Miss Fremwell!"

She opened the door a bit wider and looked. Then she slammed the door and locked it. From behind the thin paneling her voice was toneless.

"I can still see the hole, Mr. Lemon," she said.

Dark
They
Were,
and
Golden-eyed

The rocket metal cooled in the meadow winds. Its lid gave a bulging *pop*. From its clock interior stepped a man, a woman, and three children. The other passengers whispered away across the Martian meadow, leaving the man alone among his family.

The man felt his hair flutter and the tissues of his body draw tight as if he were standing at the center of a vacuum. His wife, before him, seemed almost to whirl away in smoke. The children, small seeds, might at any instant be sown to all the Martian climes.

The children looked up at him, as people look to the sun to tell what time of their life it is. His face was cold.

"What's wrong?" asked his wife.

"Let's get back on the rocket."

"Go back to Earth?"

"Yes! Listen!"

The wind blew as if to flake away their identities. At any moment the Martian air might draw his soul from him, as marrow comes from a white bone. He felt submerged in a chemical that could dissolve his intellect and burn away his past.

They looked at Martian hills that time had worn with a crushing pressure of years. They saw the old cities, lost in their meadows, lying like children's delicate bones among the blowing lakes of grass.

"Chin up, Harry," said his wife. "It's too late. We've come over sixty million miles."

The children with their yellow hair hollered at the deep dome of Martian sky. There was no answer but the racing hiss of wind through the stiff grass.

He picked up the luggage in his cold hands. "Here we go," he said—a man standing on the edge of a sea, ready to wade in and be drowned.

They walked into town.

Their name was Bittering. Harry and his wife Cora; Dan, Laura, and David. They built a small white cottage and ate good breakfasts there, but the fear was never gone. It lay with Mr. Bittering and Mrs. Bittering, a third unbidden partner at every midnight talk, at every dawn awakening.

"I feel like a salt crystal," he said, "in a mountain stream, being washed away. We don't belong here. We're Earth people. This is Mars. It was meant for Martians. For heaven's sake, Cora, let's buy tickets for home!"

But she only shook her head. "One day the atom bomb will fix Earth. Then we'll be safe here."

"Safe and insane!"

Tick-tock, seven o'clock sang the voice-clock; *time to get up.* And they did.

Something made him check everything each morning— warm hearth, potted blood-geraniums—precisely as if he expected something to be amiss. The morning paper was toast-warm from the 6 A.M. Earth rocket. He broke its seal and tilted it at his breakfast place. He forced himself to be convivial.

"Colonial days all over again," he declared. "Why, in ten years there'll be a million Earthmen on Mars. Big cities, everything! They said we'd fail. Said the Martians would resent our invasion. But did we find any Martians? Not a living soul! Oh, we found their empty cities, but no one in them. Right?"

A river of wind submerged the house. When the windows ceased rattling Mr. Bittering swallowed and looked at the children.

"I don't know," said David. "Maybe there're Martians around we don't see. Sometimes nights I think I hear 'em. I hear the wind. The sand hits my window. I get scared. And I see those towns way up in the mountains where the Martians lived a long time ago. And I think I see things moving around those towns, Papa. And I wonder if those Martians *mind* us living here. I wonder if they won't do something to us for coming here."

"Nonsense!" Mr. Bittering looked out the windows. "We're clean, decent people." He looked at his children. "All dead cities have some kind of ghosts in them. Memories, I mean." He stared at the hills. "You see a staircase and you wonder what Martians looked like climbing it. You see Martian paintings and you wonder what the painter was like. You make a little ghost in your mind, a memory. It's quite natural. Imagination." He stopped. "You haven't been prowling up in those ruins, have you?"

"No, Papa." David looked at his shoes.

"See that you stay away from them. Pass the jam."

"Just the same," said little David, "I bet something happens."

Something happened that afternoon.

Laura stumbled through the settlement, crying. She dashed blindly onto the porch.

"Mother, Father—the war, Earth!" she sobbed. "A radio flash just came. Atom bombs hit New York! All the space rockets blown up. No more rockets to Mars, ever!"

"Oh, Harry!" The mother held onto her husband and daughter.

"Are you sure, Laura?" asked the father quietly.

Laura wept. "We're stranded on Mars, forever and ever!"

For a long time there was only the sound of the wind in the late afternoon.

Alone, thought Bittering. Only a thousand of us here. No way back. No way. No way. Sweat poured from his face and his hands and his body; he was drenched in the hotness of his fear. He wanted to strike Laura, cry, "No, you're lying! The rockets will come back!" Instead, he stroked Laura's head against him and said, "The rockets will get through someday."

"Father, what will we do?"

"Go about our business, of course. Raise crops and children. Wait. Keep things going until the war ends and the rockets come again."

The two boys stepped out onto the porch.

"Children," he said, sitting there, looking beyond them, "I've something to tell you."

"We know," they said.

In the following days, Bittering wandered often through the garden to stand alone in his fear. As long as the rockets had spun a silver web across space, he had been able to accept Mars. For he had always told himself: Tomorrow, if I want, I can buy a ticket and go back to Earth.

But now: The web gone, the rockets lying in jigsaw heaps of molten girder and unsnaked wire. Earth people left to the strangeness of Mars, the cinnamon dusts and wine airs, to be baked like gingerbread shapes in Martian summers, put into harvested storage by Martian winters. What would happen to him, the others? This was the moment Mars had waited for. Now it would eat them.

He got down on his knees in the flower bed, a spade in his nervous hands. Work, he thought, work and forget.

He glanced up from the garden to the Martian mountains. He thought of the proud old Martian names that had once been on those peaks. Earthmen, dropping from the sky, had gazed upon hills, rivers, Martian seas left nameless in spite of names. Once Martians had built cities, named cities; climbed mountains, named mountains; sailed seas, named seas. Mountains melted, seas drained, cities tumbled. In spite of this, the Earthmen had felt a silent guilt at putting new names to these ancient hills and valleys.

Nevertheless, man lives by symbol and label. The names were given.

Mr. Bittering felt very alone in his garden under the Martian sun, anachronism bent here, planting Earth flowers in a wild soil.

Think. Keep thinking. Different things. Keep your mind free of Earth, the atom war, the lost rockets.

He perspired. He glanced about. No one watching. He removed his tie. Pretty bold, he thought. First your coat off, now your tie. He hung it neatly on a peach tree he had imported as a sapling from Massachusetts.

He returned to his philosophy of names and mountains. The Earthmen had changed names. Now there were Hormel Valleys, Roosevelt Seas, Ford Hills, Vanderbilt Plateaus, Rockefeller Rivers, on Mars. It wasn't right. The American settlers had shown wisdom, using old Indian prairie names: Wisconsin, Minnesota, Idaho, Ohio, Utah, Milwaukee, Waukegan, Osseo. The old names, the old meanings.

Staring at the mountains wildly, he thought: Are you up there? All the dead ones, you Martians? Well, here we are, alone, cut off! Come down, move us out! We're helpless!

The wind blew a shower of peach blossoms.

He put out his sun-browned hand, gave a small cry. He touched the blossoms, picked them up. He turned them, he touched them again and again. Then he shouted for his wife.

"Cora!"

She appeared at a window. He ran to her.

"Cora, these blossoms!"

She handled them.

"Do you see? They're different. They've changed! They're not peach blossoms any more!"

"Look all right to me," she said.

"They're not. They're *wrong!* I can't tell how. An extra petal, a leaf, something, the color, the smell!"

The children ran out in time to see their father hurrying about the garden, pulling up radishes, onions, and carrots from their beds.

"Cora, come look!"

They handled the onions, the radishes, the carrots among them.

"Do they look like carrots?"

"Yes . . . no." She hesitated. "I don't know."

"They're changed."

"Perhaps."

"You know they have! Onions but not onions, carrots but not carrots. Taste: the same but different. Smell: not like it used to be." He felt his heart pounding, and he was afraid. He dug his fingers into the earth. "Cora, what's happening? What is it? We've got to get away from this." He ran across the garden. Each tree felt his touch. "The roses. The roses. They're turning green!"

And they stood looking at the green roses.

And two days later Dan came running. "Come see the cow. I was milking her and I saw it. Come on!"

They stood in the shed and looked at their one cow. It was growing a third horn.

And the lawn in front of their house very quietly and slowly was coloring itself like spring violets. Seed from Earth but growing up a soft purple.

"We must get away," said Bittering. "We'll eat this stuff and then we'll change—who knows to what? I can't let it happen. There's only one thing to do. Burn this food!"

"It's not poisoned."

"But it is. Subtly, very subtly. A little bit. A very little bit. We mustn't touch it."

He looked with dismay at their house. "Even the house. The wind's done something to it. The air's burned it. The fog at night. The boards, all warped out of shape. It's not an Earthman's house any more."

"Oh, your imagination!"

He put on his coat and tie. "I'm going into town. We've got to do something now. I'll be back."

"Wait, Harry!" his wife cried.

But he was gone.

In town, on the shadowy step of the grocery store, the men sat with their hands on their knees, conversing with great leisure and ease.

Mr. Bittering wanted to fire a pistol in the air.

What are you doing, you fools! he thought. Sitting here! You've heard the news—we're stranded on this planet. Well, move! Aren't you frightened? Aren't you afraid? What are you going to do?

"Hello, Harry," said everyone.

"Look," he said to them. "You did hear the news, the other day, didn't you?"

They nodded and laughed. "Sure. Sure, Harry."

"What are you going to do about it?"

"Do, Harry, do? What *can* we do?"

"Build a rocket, that's what!"

"A rocket, Harry? To go back to all that trouble? Oh, Harry!"

"But you *must* want to go back. Have you noticed the peach blossoms, the onions, the grass?"

"Why, yes, Harry, seems we did," said one of the men.

"Doesn't it scare you?"

"Can't recall that it did much, Harry."

"Idiots!"

"Now, Harry."

Bittering wanted to cry. "You've got to work with me. If we stay here, we'll all change. The air. Don't you smell it? Something in the air. A Martian virus, maybe; some seed, or a pollen. Listen to me!"

They stared at him.

"Sam," he said to one of them.

"Yes, Harry?"

"Will you help me build a rocket?"

"Harry, I got a whole load of metal and some blueprints. You want to work in my metal shop on a rocket, you're welcome. I'll sell you that metal for five hundred dollars. You should be able to construct a right pretty rocket, if you work alone, in about thirty years."

Everyone laughed.

"Don't laugh."

Sam looked at him with quiet good humor.

"Sam," Bittering said. "Your eyes——"

"What about them, Harry?"

"Didn't they used to be grey?"

"Well now, I don't remember."

"They were, weren't they?"

"Why do you ask, Harry?"

"Because now they're kind of yellow-colored."

"Is that so, Harry?" Sam said, casually.

"And you're taller and thinner——"

"You might be right, Harry."

"Sam, you shouldn't have yellow eyes."

"Harry, what color eyes have *you* got?" Sam said.

"My eyes? They're blue, of course."

"Here you are, Harry." Sam handed him a pocket mirror. "Take a look at yourself."

Mr. Bittering hesitated, and then raised the mirror to his face.

There were little, very dim flecks of new gold captured in the blue of his eyes.

"Now look what you've done," said Sam a moment later. "You've broken my mirror."

Harry Bittering moved into the metal shop and began to build the rocket. Men stood in the open door and talked and joked without raising their voices. Once in a while they gave him a hand on lifting something. But mostly they just idled and watched him with their yellowing eyes.

"It's suppertime, Harry," they said.

His wife appeared with his supper in a wicker basket.

"I won't touch it," he said. "I'll eat only food from our Deepfreeze. Food that came from Earth. Nothing from our garden."

His wife stood watching him. "You can't build a rocket."

"I worked in a shop once, when I was twenty. I know metal. Once I get it started, the others will help," he said, not looking at her, laying out the blueprints.

"Harry, Harry," she said, helplessly.

"We've got to get away, Cora. We've *got* to!"

The nights were full of wind that blew down the empty moonlit sea meadows past the little white chess cities lying for their twelve-thousandth year in the shallows. In the Earthmen's settlement, the Bittering house shook with a feeling of change.

Lying abed, Mr. Bittering felt his bones shifted, shaped, melted like gold. His wife, lying beside him, was dark from many sunny afternoons. Dark she was, and golden-eyed, burnt almost black by the sun, sleeping, and the children metallic in their beds, and the wind roaring forlorn and changing through the old peach trees, the violet grass, shaking out green rose petals.

The fear would not be stopped. It had his throat and heart. It dripped in a wetness of the arm and the temple and the trembling palm.

A green star rose in the east.

A strange word emerged from Mr. Bittering's lips.

"*Iorrt. Iorrt.*" He repeated it.

It was a Martian word. He knew no Martian.

In the middle of the night he arose and dialed a call through to Simpson, the archeologist.

"Simpson, what does the word *Iorrt* mean?"

"Why that's the old Martian word for our planet Earth. Why?"

"No special reason."

The telephone slipped from his hand.

"Hello, hello, hello, hello," it kept saying while he sat gazing out at the green star. "Bittering? Harry, are you there?"

The days were full of metal sound. He laid the frame of the rocket with the reluctant help of three indifferent men. He grew very tired in an hour or so and had to sit down.

"The altitude," laughed a man.

"Are you *eating*, Harry?" asked another.

"I'm eating," he said, angrily.

"From your Deepfreeze?"

"Yes!"

"You're getting thinner, Harry."

"I'm not!"

"And taller."

"Liar!"

His wife took him aside a few days later. "Harry, I've used up all the food in the Deepfreeze. There's nothing left. I'll have to make sandwiches using food grown on Mars."

He sat down heavily.

"You must eat," she said. "You're weak."

"Yes," he said.

He took a sandwich, opened it, looked at it, and began to nibble at it.

"And take the rest of the day off," she said. "It's hot. The children want to swim in the canals and hike. Please come along."

"I can't waste time. This is a crisis!"

"Just for an hour," she urged. "A swim'll do you good."

He rose, sweating. "All right, all right. Leave me alone. I'll come."

"Good for you, Harry."

The sun was hot, the day quiet. There was only an immense staring burn upon the land. They moved along the canal, the father, the mother, the racing children in their swim suits. They stopped and ate meat sandwiches. He saw their skin baking brown. And he saw the yellow eyes of his wife and his children, their eyes that were never yellow before. A few tremblings shook him, but were carried off in waves of pleasant heat as he lay in the sun. He was too tired to be afraid.

"Cora, how long have your eyes been yellow?"

She was bewildered. "Always, I guess."

"They didn't change from brown in the last three months?"

She bit her lips. "No. Why do you ask?"

"Never mind."

They sat there.

"The children's eyes," he said. "They're yellow, too."

"Sometimes growing children's eyes change color."

"Maybe *we're* children, too. At least to Mars. That's a thought." He laughed. "Think I'll swim."

They leaped into the canal water, and he let himself sink down and down to the bottom like a golden statue and lie there in green silence. All was water-quiet and deep, all was peace. He felt the steady, slow current drift him easily.

If I lie here long enough, he thought, the water will work and eat away my flesh until the bones show like coral. Just my skeleton left. And then the water can build on that skeleton—green things, deep water things, red things, yellow things. Change. Change. Slow, deep, silent change. And isn't that what it is up *there?*

He saw the sky submerged above him, the sun made Martian by atmosphere and time and space.

Up there, a big river, he thought, a Martian river, all of us lying deep in it, in our pebble houses, in our sunken boulder houses, like crayfish hidden, and the water washing away our old bodies and lengthening the bones and——

He let himself drift up through the soft light.

Dan sat on the edge of the canal, regarding his father seriously.

"*Utha,*" he said.

"What?" asked his father.

The boy smiled. "You know. *Utha's* the Martian word for 'father.' "

"Where did you learn it?"

"I don't know. Around. *Utha!*"

"What do you want?"

The boy hesitated. "I—I want to change my name."

"Change it?"

"Yes."

His mother swam over. "What's wrong with Dan for a name?"

Dan fidgeted. "The other day you called Dan, Dan, Dan. I didn't even hear. I said to myself, That's not my name. I've a new name I want to use."

Mr. Bittering held to the side of the canal, his body cold and his heart pounding slowly. "What is this new name?"

"Linnl. Isn't that a good name? Can I use it? Can't I, please?"

Mr. Bittering put his hand to his head. He thought of the silly rocket, himself working alone, himself alone even among his family, so alone.

He heard his wife say, "Why not?"

He heard himself say, "Yes, you can use it."

"Yaaa!" screamed the boy. "I'm Linnl, Linnl!"

Racing down the meadowlands, he danced and shouted.

Mr. Bittering looked at his wife. "Why did we do that?"

"I don't know," she said. "It just seemed like a good idea."

They walked into the hills. They strolled on old mosaic paths, beside still pumping fountains. The paths were covered with a thin film of cool water all summer long. You kept your bare feet cool all the day, splashing as in a creek, wading.

They came to a small deserted Martian villa with a good view of the valley. It was on top of a hill. Blue marble halls, large murals, a swimming pool. It was refreshing in this hot summertime. The Martians hadn't believed in large cities.

"How nice," said Mrs. Bittering, "if we could move up here to this villa for the summer."

"Come on," he said. "We're going back to town. There's work to be done on the rocket."

But as he worked that night, the thought of the cool blue marble villa entered his mind. As the hours passed, the rocket seemed less important.

In the flow of days and weeks, the rocket receded and dwindled. The old fever was gone. It frightened him to think he had let it slip this way. But somehow the heat, the air, the working conditions——

He heard the men murmuring on the porch of his metal shop.

"Everyone's going. You heard?"

"All going. That's right."

Bittering came out. "Going where?" He saw a couple of trucks, loaded with children and furniture, drive down the dusty street.

"Up to the villas," said the man.

"Yeah, Harry. I'm going. So is Sam. Aren't you, Sam?"

"That's right, Harry. What about you?"

"I've got work to do here."

"Work! You can finish that rocket in the autumn, when it's cooler."

He took a breath. "I got the frame all set up."

"In the autumn is better." Their voices were lazy in the heat.

"Got to work," he said.

"Autumn," they reasoned. And they sounded so sensible, so right.

"Autumn would be best," he thought. "Plenty of time, then."

No! cried part of himself, deep down, put away, locked tight, suffocating. No! No!

"In the autumn," he said.

"Come on, Harry," they all said.

"Yes," he said, feeling his flesh melt in the hot liquid air. "Yes, in the autumn. I'll begin work again then."

"I got a villa near the Tirra Canal," said someone.

"You mean the Roosevelt Canal, don't you?"

"Tirra. The old Martian name."

"But on the map——"

"Forget the map. It's Tirra now. Now I found a place in the Pillan mountains—"

"You mean the Rockefeller range," said Bittering.

"I mean the Pillan mountains," said Sam.

"Yes," said Bittering, buried in the hot, swarming air. "The Pillan mountains."

Everyone worked at loading the truck in the hot, still afternoon of the next day.

Laura, Dan, and David carried packages. Or, as they preferred to be known, Ttil, Linnl, and Werr carried packages.

The furniture was abandoned in the little white cottage.

"It looked just fine in Boston," said the mother. "And here in the cottage. But up at the villa? No. We'll get it when we come back in the autumn."

Bittering himself was quiet.

"I've some ideas on furniture for the villa," he said after a time. "Big, lazy furniture."

"What about your encyclopedia? You're taking it along, surely?"

Mr. Bittering glanced away. "I'll come and get it next week."

They turned to their daughter. "What about your New York dresses?"

The bewildered girl stared. "Why, I don't want them any more."

They shut off the gas, the water, they locked the doors and walked away. Father peered into the truck.

"Gosh, we're not taking much," he said. "Considering all we brought to Mars, this is only a handful!"

He started the truck.

Looking at the small white cottage for a long moment, he was filled with a desire to rush to it, touch it, say good-by to it, for he felt as if he were going away on a long journey, leaving something to which he could never quite return, never understand again.

Just then Sam and his family drove by in another truck.

"Hi, Bittering! Here we go!"

The truck swung down the ancient highway out of town. There were sixty others traveling the same direction. The town filled with a silent, heavy dust from their passage. The canal waters lay blue in the sun, and a quiet wind moved in the strange trees.

"Good-by, town!" said Mr. Bittering.

"Good-by, good-by," said the family, waving to it.

They did not look back again.

Summer burned the canals dry. Summer moved like flame upon the meadows. In the empty Earth settlement, the painted houses flaked and peeled. Rubber tires upon which children had swung in back yards hung suspended like stopped clock pendulums in the blazing air.

At the metal shop, the rocket frame began to rust.

In the quiet autumn Mr. Bittering stood, very dark now, very golden-eyed, upon the slope above his villa, looking at the valley.

"It's time to go back," said Cora.

"Yes, but we're not going," he said quietly. "There's nothing there any more."

"Your books," she said. "Your fine clothes."

"Your *lles* and your fine *ior uele rre*," she said.

"The town's empty. No one's going back," he said. "There's no reason to, none at all."

The daughter wove tapestries and the sons played songs on ancient flutes and pipes, their laughter echoing in the marble villa.

Mr. Bittering gazed at the Earth settlement far away in the low valley. "Such odd, such ridiculous houses the Earth people built."

"They didn't know any better," his wife mused. "Such ugly people. I'm glad they've gone."

They both looked at each other, startled by all they had just finished saying. They laughed.

"Where did they go?" he wondered. He glanced at his wife. She was golden and slender as his daughter. She looked at him, and he seemed almost as young as their eldest son.

"I don't know," she said.

"We'll go back to town maybe next year, or the year after, or the year after that," he said, calmly. "Now—I'm warm. How about taking a swim?"

They turned their backs to the valley. Arm in arm they walked silently down a path of clear-running spring water.

Five years later a rocket fell out of the sky. It lay steaming in the valley. Men leaped out of it, shouting.

"We won the war on Earth! We're here to rescue you! Hey!"

But the American-built town of cottages, peach trees, and theaters was silent. They found a flimsy rocket frame rusting in an empty shop.

The rocket men searched the hills. The captain established headquarters in an abandoned bar. His lieutenant came back to report.

"The town's empty, but we found native life in the hills, sir. Dark people. Yellow eyes. Martians. Very friendly. We talked a bit, not much. They learn English fast. I'm sure our relations will be most friendly with them, sir."

"Dark, eh?" mused the captain. "How many?"

"Six, eight hundred, I'd say, living in those marble ruins in the hills, sir. Tall, healthy. Beautiful women."

"Did they tell you what became of the men and women who built this Earth-settlement, Lieutenant?"

"They hadn't the foggiest notion of what happened to this town or its people."

"Strange. You think those Martians killed them?"

"They look surprisingly peaceful. Chances are a plague did this town in, sir."

"Perhaps. I suppose this is one of those mysteries we'll never solve. One of those mysteries you read about."

The captain looked at the room, the dusty windows, the blue mountains rising beyond, the canals moving in the light, and he heard the soft wind in the air. He shivered. Then, recovering, he tapped a large fresh map he had thumbtacked to the top of an empty table.

"Lots to be done, Lieutenant." His voice droned on and quietly on as the sun sank behind the blue hills. "New settlements. Mining sites, minerals to be looked for. Bacteriological specimens taken. The work, all the work. And the old records were lost. We'll have a job of remapping to do, renaming the mountains and rivers and such. Calls for a little imagination.

"What do you think of naming those mountains the Lincoln Mountains, this canal the Washington Canal, those hills—we can name those hills for you, Lieutenant. Diplomacy. And you, for a favor, might name a town for me. Polishing the apple. And why not make this the Einstein Valley, and further over . . . are you *listening*, Lieutenant?"

The lieutenant snapped his gaze from the blue color and the quiet mist of the hills far beyond the town.

"What? Oh, *yes*, sir!"

The
Smile

In the town square the queue had formed at five in the morning while cocks were crowing far out in the rimed country and there were no fires. All about, among the ruined buildings, bits of mist had clung at first, but now with the new light of seven o'clock it was beginning to disperse. Down the road, in twos and threes, more people were gathering in for the day of marketing, the day of festival.

The small boy stood immediately behind two men who had been talking loudly in the clear air, and all of the sounds they made seemed twice as loud because of the cold. The small boy stomped his feet and blew on his red, chapped hands, and looked up at the soiled gunny-sack clothing of the men and down the long line of men and women ahead.

"Here, boy, what're you doing out so early?" said the man behind him.

"Got my place in line, I have," said the boy.

"Whyn't you run off, give your place to someone who appreciates?"

"Leave the boy alone," said the man ahead, suddenly turning.

"I was joking." The man behind put his hand on the

110

boy's head. The boy shook it away coldly. "I just thought it strange, a boy out of bed so early."

"This boy's an appreciator of arts, I'll have you know," said the boy's defender, a man named Grigsby. "What's your name, lad?"

"Tom."

"Tom here is going to spit clean and true, right, Tom?"

"I sure am!"

Laughter passed down the line.

A man was selling cracked cups of hot coffee up ahead. Tom looked and saw the little hot fire and the brew bubbling in a rusty pan. It wasn't really coffee. It was made from some berry that grew on the meadowlands beyond town, and it sold a penny a cup to warm their stomachs; but not many were buying, not many had the wealth.

Tom stared ahead to the place where the line ended, beyond a bombed-out stone wall.

"They say she *smiles*," said the boy.

"Aye, she does," said Grigsby.

"They say she's made of oil and canvas."

"True. And that's what makes me think she's not the original one. The original, now, I've heard, was painted on wood a long time ago."

"They say she's four centuries old."

"Maybe more. No one knows what year this is, to be sure."

"It's 2061!"

"That's what they say, boy, yes. Liars. Could be 3000 or 5000, for all we know. Things were in a fearful mess there for a while. All we got now is bits and pieces."

They shuffled along the cold stones of the street.

"How much longer before we see her?" asked Tom uneasily.

"Just a few more minutes. They got her set up with four brass poles and velvet rope, all fancy, to keep folks back. Now mind, no rocks, Tom; they don't allow rocks thrown at her."

"Yes, sir."

The sun rose higher in the heavens, bringing heat which made the men shed their grimy coats and greasy hats.

"Why're we all here in line?" asked Tom at last. "Why're we all here to spit?"

Grigsby did not glance down at him, but judged the sun. "Well, Tom, there's lots of reasons." He reached absently for a pocket that was long gone, for a cigarette that wasn't there. Tom had seen the gesture a million times. "Tom, it has to do with hate. Hate for everything in the Past. I ask you, Tom, how did we get in such a state, cities all junk, roads like jigsaws from bombs, and half the cornfields glowing with radio-activity at night? Ain't that a lousy stew, I ask you?"

"Yes, sir, I guess so."

"It's this way, Tom. You hate whatever it was that got you all knocked down and ruined. That's human nature. Unthinking, maybe, but human nature anyway."

"There's hardly nobody or nothing we don't hate," said Tom.

"Right! The whole blooming kaboodle of them people in the Past who run the world. So here we are on a Thursday morning with our guts plastered to our spines, cold, live in caves and such, don't smoke, don't drink, don't nothing except have our festivals, Tom, our festivals."

And Tom thought of the festivals in the past few years. The year they tore up all the books in the square and burned them and everyone was drunk and laughing. And the festival of science a month ago when they dragged in the last motorcar and picked lots and each lucky man who won was allowed one smash of a sledge hammer at the car.

"Do I remember *that,* Tom? Do I *remember?* Why, I got to smash the front window, the window, you hear? My God, it made a lovely sound! *Crash!*"

Tom could hear the glass fall in glittering heaps.

"And Bill Henderson, he got to bash the engine. Oh, he did a smart job of it, with great efficiency. Wham!"

"But best of all," recalled Grigsby, "there was the time they smashed a factory that was still trying to turn out airplanes.

"Lord, did we feel good blowing it up!" said Grigsby. "And than we found that newspaper plant and the munitions depot and exploded them together. Do you understand, Tom?"

Tom puzzled over it. "I guess."

It was high noon. Now the odors of the ruined city

stank on the hot air and things crawled among the tumbled buildings.

"Won't it ever come back, mister?"

"What, civilization? Nobody wants it. Not me!"

"I could stand a bit of it," said the man behind another man. "There were a few spots of beauty in it."

"Don't worry your heads," shouted Grigsby. "There's no room for that, either."

"Ah," said the man behind the man. "Someone'll come along someday with imagination and patch it up. Mark my words. Someone with a heart."

"No," said Grigsby.

"I say yes. Someone with a soul for pretty things. Might give us back a kind of *limited* sort of civilization, the kind we could live in in peace."

"First thing you know there's war!"

"But maybe next time it'd be different."

At last they stood in the main square. A man on horseback was riding from the distance into the town. He had a piece of paper in his hand. In the center of the square was the roped-off area. Tom, Grigsby, and the others were collecting their spittle and moving forward—moving forward prepared and ready, eyes wide. Tom felt his heart beating very strongly and excitedly, and the earth was hot under his bare feet.

"Here we go, Tom, let fly!"

Four policemen stood at the corners of the roped area, four men with bits of yellow twine on their wrists to show their authority over other men. They were there to prevent rocks being hurled.

"This way," said Grigsby at the last moment, "everyone feels he's had his chance at her, you see, Tom? Go on, now!"

Tom stood before the painting and looked at it for a long time.

"Tom, spit!"

His mouth was dry.

"Get on, Tom! Move!"

"But," said Tom, slowly, "she's *beautiful!*"

"Here, I'll spit for you!" Grigsby spat and the missile flew in the sunlight. The woman in the portrait smiled serenely, secretly, at Tom, and he looked back at her, his heart beating, a kind of music in his ears.

"She's beautiful," he said.

"Now get on, before the police———"

"Attention!"

The line fell silent. One moment they were berating Tom for not moving forward, now they were turning to the man on horseback.

"What do they call it, sir?" asked Tom, quietly.

"The picture? *Mona Lisa,* Tom, I think. Yes, the *Mona Lisa.*"

"I have an announcement," said the man on horseback. "The authorities have decreed that as of high noon today the portrait in the square is to be given over into the hands of the populace there, so they may participate in the destruction of———"

Tom hadn't even time to scream before the crowd bore him, shouting and pummeling about, stampeding toward the portrait. There was a sharp ripping sound. The police ran to escape. The crowd was in full cry, their hands like so many hungry birds pecking away at the portrait. Tom felt himself thrust almost through the broken thing. Reaching out in blind imitation of the others, he snatched a scrap of oily canvas, yanked, felt the canvas give, then fell, was kicked, sent rolling to the outer rim of the mob. Bloody, his clothing torn, he watched old women chew pieces of canvas, men break the frame, kick the ragged cloth, and rip it into confetti.

Only Tom stood apart, silent in the moving square. He looked down at his hand. It clutched the piece of canvas close to his chest, hidden.

"Hey there, Tom!" cried Grigsby.

Without a word, sobbing, Tom ran. He ran out and down the bomb-pitted road, into a field, across a shallow stream, not looking back, his hand clenched tightly, tucked under his coat.

At sunset he reached the small village and passed on through. By nine o'clock he came to the ruined farm dwelling. Around back, in the half silo, in the part that still remained upright, tented over, he heard the sounds of sleeping, the family—his mother, father, and brother. He slipped quickly, silently, through the small door and lay down, panting.

"Tom?" called his mother in the dark.

"Yes."

"Where've you been?" snapped his father. "I'll beat you in the morning."

Someone kicked him. His brother, who had been left behind to work their little patch of ground.

"Go to sleep," cried his mother, faintly.

Another kick.

Tom lay getting his breath. All was quiet. His hand was pushed to his chest, tight, tight. He lay for half an hour this way, eyes closed.

Then he felt something, and it was a cold white light. The moon rose very high and the little square of light moved in the silo and crept slowly over Tom's body. Then, and only then, did his hand relax. Slowly, carefully, listening to those who slept about him, Tom drew his hand forth. He hesitated, sucked in his breath, and then, waiting, opened his hand and uncrumpled the tiny fragment of painted canvas.

All the world was asleep in the moonlight.

And there on his hand was the Smile.

He looked at it in the white illumination from the midnight sky. And he thought, over and over to himself, quietly, *the Smile, the lovely Smile.*

An hour later he could still see it, even after he had folded it carefully and hidden it. He shut his eyes and the Smile was there in the darkness. And it was still there, warm and gentle, when he went to sleep and the world was silent and the moon sailed up and then down the cold sky toward morning.

The
First
Night
of
Lent

So you want to know all the whys and wherefores of the Irish? What shapes them to their Dooms and runs them on their way? you ask. Well, listen, then. For though I've known but a single Irishman in all my life, I knew him, without pause, for one hundred and forty-four consecutive nights. Stand close; perhaps in him you'll see that entire race which marches out of the rains but to vanish through the mists; hold on, here they come! Look out, there they go!

This Irishman, his name was Nick.

During the autumn of 1953, I began a screenplay in Dublin, and each afternoon a hired cab drove me thirty miles out from the River Liffey to the huge grey Georgian country house where my producer-director rode to hounds. There, we discussed my eight pages of daily script through the long fall, winter, and early spring evenings. Then, each midnight, ready to turn back to the Irish Sea and the Royal Hibernian Hotel, I'd wake the operator in the Kilcock village exchange and have her put me through to the warmest, if totally unheated, spot in town.

"Heber Finn's pub?" I'd shout, once connected. "Is Nick there? Could you send him along here, please?"

My mind's eye saw them, the local boys, lined up, peering over the barricade at that freckled mirror so like a frozen winter pond and themselves discovered all drowned and deep under that lovely ice. Amid all their jostlings and their now-here's-a-secret-in-a-stage-whisper-commotion stood Nick, my village driver, his quietness abounding. I heard Heber Finn sing out from the phone. I heard Nick start up and reply:

"Just look at me, headin' for the door!"

Early on, I learned that "headin' for the door" was no nerve-shattering process that might affront dignity or destroy the fine filigree of any argument being woven with great and breathless beauty at Heber Finn's. It was, rather, a gradual disengagement, a leaning of the bulk so one's gravity was diplomatically shifted toward that far empty side of the public room where the door, shunned by all, stood neglected. Meantime, a dozen conversational warps and woofs must be ticked, tied, and labeled so next morn, with hoarse cries of recognition, patterns might be seized and the shuttle thrown with no pause for breath or thought.

Timing it, I figured the long part of Nick's midnight journey—the length of Heber Finn's—took half an hour. The short part—from Finn's to the house where I waited—took but five minutes.

So it was on the night before the first night of Lent. I called. I waited.

And at last, down through the night forest, thrashed the 1931 Chevrolet, peat-turf colored on top like Nick. Car and driver gasped, sighed, wheezed softly, easily, gently as they nudged into the courtyard and I groped down the front steps under a moonless but brightly starred sky.

I peered through the car window at unstirred dark; the dashboard had been dead these many years.

"Nick . . . ?"

"None other," he whispered secretly. "And ain't it a fine warm evenin'?"

The temperature was fifty. But, Nick'd been no nearer Rome than the Tipperary shore line; so weather was relative.

"A fine warm evening." I climbed up front and gave the squealing door its absolutely compulsory, rust-splintering slam. "Nick, how've you been since?"

"Ah." He let the car bulk and grind itself down the forest path. "I got me health. Ain't that all-and-everything with Lent comin' on tomorra?"

"Lent," I mused. "What will you give up for Lent, Nick?"

"I been turnin' it over." Nick sucked his cigarette suddenly; the pink, lined mask of his face blinked off the smoke. "And why not these terrible things ya see in me mouth? Dear as gold-fillin's, and a dread congestor of the lungs they be. Put it all down, add 'em up, and ya got a sick loss by the year's turnin', ya know. So ya'll not find these filthy creatures in me face again the whole time of Lent, and, who knows, after!"

"Bravo!" said I, a non-smoker.

"Bravo, says I to meself," wheezed Nick, one eye flinched with smoke.

"Good luck," I said.

"I'll need it," whispered Nick, "with the Sin's own habit to be broke."

And we moved with firm control, with thoughtful shift of weight, down and around a turfy hollow and through a mist and into Dublin at thirty-one easy miles an hour.

Bear with me while I stress it: Nick was the most careful driver in all God's world, including any sane, small, quiet, butter-and-milk producing country you name.

Above all, Nick stands innocent and sainted when compared to those motorists who key that small switch marked paranoia each time they fuse themselves to their bucket seats in Los Angeles, Mexico City, or Paris. Also, to those blind men who, forsaking tin cups and canes, but still wearing their Hollywood dark-glasses, laugh insanely down the Via Veneto, shaking brake-drum lining like carnival serpentine out their race-car windows. Consider the Roman ruins; surely they are the wreckage strewn and left by those motor-biking otters who, all night beneath your hotel window, shriek down dark Roman alleys, Christians hell-bent for the Colosseum lion pits.

Nick, now. See his easy hands loving the wheel in a slow clock-like turning as soft and silent as winter constellations snow down the sky. Listen to his mist-breathing voice all night-quiet as he charms the road, his foot a tenderly benevolent pat on the whispering accelerator, never a mile under thirty, never two miles over. Nick, Nick, and his steady boat gentling a mild sweet lake where all Time slumbers. Look, compare. And bind such a man to you with summer grasses, gift him with silver, shake his hand warmly at each journey's end.

"Good night, Nick," I said at the hotel. "See you tomorrow."

"God willing," whispered Nick.

And he drove softly away.

Let twenty-three hours of sleep, breakfast, lunch, supper, late night-cap pass. Let hours of writing bad script into fair script fade to peat mist and rain, and there I come again, another midnight, out of that Georgian mansion, its door throwing a warm hearth of color before me as I tread down the steps to feel Braille-wise in fog for the car I know hulks there; I hear its enlarged and asthmatic heart gasping in the blind air, and Nick coughing his "gold by the ounce is not more precious" cough.

"Ah, there you are, sir!" said Nick.

And I climbed in the sociable front seat and gave the door its slam. "Nick," I said, smiling.

And then the impossible happened. The car jerked as if shot from the blazing mouth of a cannon, roared, took off, bounced, skidded, then cast itself in full, stoning ricochet down the path among shattered bushes and writhing shadows. I snatched my knees as my head hit the car top four times.

Nick! I almost shouted. Nick!

Visions of Los Angeles, Mexico City, Paris, jumped through my mind. I gazed in frank dismay at the speedometer. Eighty, ninety, one hundred kilometers; we shot out a great blast of gravel behind and hit the main road, rocked over a bridge and slid down in the midnight streets of Kilcock. No sooner in than out of town at one hundred ten kilometers, I felt all Ireland's grass put down its ears when we, with a yell, jumped over a rise.

Nick! I thought, and turned, and there he sat, only one thing the same. On his lips a cigarette burned, blinding first one eye, then the other.

But the rest of Nick, behind the cigarette, was changed

as if the Adversary himself had squeezed and molded and fired him with a dark hand. There he was, whirling the wheel round-about, over-around; here we frenzied under trestles, out of tunnels, here knocked crossroad signs spinning like weathercocks in whirlwinds.

Nick's face; the wisdom was drained from it, the eyes neither gentle nor philosophical, the mouth neither tolerant, nor at peace. It was a face washed raw, a scalded, peeled potato, a face more like a blinding searchlight raking its steady and meaningless glare ahead while his quick hands snaked and bit and bit the wheel again to lean us round curves and jump us off cliff after cliff of night.

It's not Nick, I thought, it's his brother. Or a dire thing's come in his life, some destroying affliction or blow, a family sorrow or sickness, yes, that's the answer.

And then Nick spoke, and his voice, it was changed too. Gone was the mellow peat bog, the moist sod, the warm fire in out of the cold rain, gone the gentle grass. Now the voice fairly cracked at me, a clarion, a trumpet, all iron and tin.

"Well, how ya been since!" Nick shouted. "How is it with ya!" he cried.

And the car, it too had suffered violence. It protested the change, yes, for it was an old and much-beaten thing that had done its time and now only wished to stroll along, like a crusty beggar toward sea and sky, careful of its breath and bones. But Nick would have none of that, and cadged the wreck on as if thundering toward Hell, there to warm his cold hands at some special blaze. Nick leaned, the car leaned; great livid gases blew out in fireworks from the exhaust. Nick's frame, my frame, the car's frame, all together, were wracked and shuddered and ticked wildly.

My sanity was saved from being torn clean off the bone by a simple act. My eyes, seeking the cause of our plaguing flight, ran over the man blazing here like a sheet of ignited vapor from the Abyss, and laid hands to the answering clue.

"Nick," I gasped, "it's the first night of Lent!"

"So?" Nick said, surprised.

"So," I said, "remembering your Lenten promise, why's that cigarette in your mouth?"

Nick did not know what I meant for a moment. Then he cast his eyes down, saw the jiggling smoke, and shrugged.

"Ah," he said, "I give up the *other*."

And suddenly it all came clear.

The other one hundred forty odd nights, at the door of the old Georgian house I had accepted from my employer a fiery douse of scotch or bourbon or some-such drink "against the chill." Then, breathing summer wheat or barley or oats or whatever from my scorched and charcoaled mouth, I had walked out to a cab where sat a man who, during all the long evenings' wait for me to phone for his services, had *lived* in Heber Finn's pub.

Fool! I thought, how could you have forgotten this!

And there in Heber Finn's, during the long hours of lacy talk that was like planting and bringing to crop a garden among busy men, each contributing his seed or flower, and wielding the implements, their tongues, and the raised, foam-hived glasses, their own hands softly curled about the dear drinks, there Nick had taken into himself a mellowness.

And that mellowness had distilled itself down in a slow rain that damped his smoldering nerves and put the wilderness fires in every limb of him out. Those same showers laved his face to leave the tidal marks of wisdom, the lines of Plato and Aeschylus there. The harvest mellowness colored his cheeks, warmed his eyes soft, lowered his voice to a husking mist, and spread in his chest to slow his heart to a gentle jog trot. It rained out his arms to loosen his hard-mouthed hands on the shuddering wheel and sit him with grace and ease in his horse-hair saddle as he gentled us through the fogs that kept us and Dublin apart.

And with the malt on my own tongue, fluming up my sinus with burning vapors, I had never detected the scent of any spirits on my old friend here.

"Ah," said Nick again. "Yes; I give up the *other*."

The last bit of jigsaw fell in place.

Tonight, the first night of Lent.

Tonight, for the first time in all the nights I had driven with him, Nick was sober.

All those other one hundred and forty-odd nights, Nick hadn't been driving careful and easy just for my safety, no, but because of the gentle weight of mellowness sloping now on this side, now on that side of him as we took the long, scything curves.

Oh, who really knows the Irish, say I, and which half of them is which? Nick?—who is Nick?—and what in the world is he? Which Nick's the real Nick, the one that everyone knows?

I will not think on it!

There is only *one* Nick for me. The one that Ireland shaped herself with her weathers and waters, her seedings and harvestings, her brans and mashes, her brews, bottlings, and ladlings-out, her summer-grain-colored pubs astir and adance with the wind in the wheat and barley by night, you may hear the good whisper way out in forest, on bog, as you roll by. That's Nick to the teeth, eye, and heart, to his easygoing hands. If you ask what makes the Irish what they are, I'd point on down the road and tell where you turn to Heber Finn's.

The first night of Lent, and before you count nine, we're in Dublin! I'm out of the cab and it's puttering there at the curb and I lean in to put my money in the hands of my driver. Earnestly, pleadingly, warmly, with all the friendly urging in the world, I look into that fine man's raw, strange, torchlike face.

"Nick," I said.

"Sir!" he shouted.

"Do me a favor," I said.

"Anything!" he shouted.

"Take this extra money," I said, "and buy the biggest bottle of Irish moss you can find. And just before you pick me up tomorrow night, Nick, drink it down, drink it all. Will you do that, Nick? Will you promise me, cross your heart and hope to die, to do that?"

He thought on it, and the very thought damped down the ruinous blaze in his face.

"Ya make it terrible hard on me," he said.

I forced his fingers shut on the money. At last he put it in his pocket and faced silently ahead.

"Good night, Nick," I said. "See you tomorrow."

"God willing," said Nick.

And he drove away.

The
Time
of
Going
Away

The thought was three days and three nights growing. During the days he carried it like a ripening peach in his head. During the nights he let it take flesh and sustenance, hung out on the silent air, colored by country moon and country stars. He walked around and around the thought in the silence before dawn. On the fourth morning he reached up an invisible hand, picked it, and swallowed it whole.

He arose as swiftly as possible and burned all his old letters, packed a few clothes in a very small case, and put on his midnight suit and a tie the shiny color of ravens' feathers, as if he were in mourning. He sensed his wife in the door behind him watching his little play with the eyes of a critic who may leap on stage any moment and stop the show. When he brushed past her, he murmured, "Excuse me."

"Excuse me!" she cried. "Is that all you say? Creeping around here, planning a trip!"

"I didn't plan it; it happened," he said. "Three days ago I got this premonition. I knew I was going to die."

"Stop that kind of talk," she said. "It makes me nervous."

The horizon was mirrored softly in his eyes. "I hear my blood running slow. Listening to my bones is like

124

standing in an attic hearing the beams shift and the dust settle."

"You're only seventy-five," said his wife. "You stand on your own two legs, see, hear, eat, and sleep good, don't you? What's all this talk?"

"It's the natural tongue of existence speaking to me," said the old man. "Civilization's got us too far away from our natural selves. Now you take the pagan island-ers——"

"I won't!"

"Everyone knows the pagan islanders got a feel for when it's time to die. They walk around shaking hands with friends and give away all their earthly goods——"

"Don't their wives have a say?"

"They give some of their earthly goods to their wives."

"I should think so!"

"And some to their friends——"

"I'll argue that!"

"And some to their friends. Then they paddle their canoes off into the sunset and never return."

His wife looked high up along him as if he were timber ripe for cutting. "Desertion!" she said.

"No, no, Mildred; death, pure and simple. The Time of Going Away, they call it."

"Did anyone ever charter a canoe and follow to see what those fools were up to?"

"Of course not," said the old man, mildly irritated. "That would spoil everything."

"You mean they had other wives and pretty friends off on another island?"

"No, no, it's just a man needs aloneness, serenity, when his juices turn cold."

"If you could prove those fools really died, I'd shut up." His wife squinted one eye. "Anyone ever *find* their bones on those far islands?"

"The fact is that they just sail on into the sunset, like animals who sense the Great Time at hand. Beyond that, I don't wish to know."

"Well, *I* know," said the old woman. "You been reading more articles in the *National Geographic* about the Elephants' Boneyard."

"Graveyard, not Boneyard!" he shouted.

"Graveyard, Boneyard. I thought I burned those magazines; you got some hid?"

"Look here, Mildred," he said severely, seizing the suitcase again. "My mind points north; nothing you say can head me south. I'm tuned to the infinite secret wellsprings of the primitive soul."

"You're tuned to whatever you read last in that bogtrotters' gazette!" She pointed a finger at him. "You think I got no memory?"

His shoulders fell. "Let's not go through the list again, please."

"What about the hairy mammoth episode?" she asked. "When they found that frozen elephant in the Russian tundra thirty years back? You and Sam Hertz, that old fool, with your fine idea of running off to Siberia to corner the world market in canned edible hairy mammoth? You think I don't still hear you saying, 'Imagine the prices members of the National Geographic Society will pay to have the tender meat of the Siberian hairy mammoth, ten thousand years old, ten thousand years extinct, right in their homes!' You think my scars have healed from that?"

"I see them clearly," he said.

"You think I've forgotten the time you went out to find the Lost Tribe of the Osseos, or whatever, in Wisconsin some place where you could dogtrot to town Saturday nights and tank up, and fell in that quarry and broke your leg and laid there three nights?"

"Your recall," he said, "is total."

"Then what's this about pagan natives and the Time of Going Away? I'll tell you what it is—it's the Time of Staying at Home! It's the time when fruit don't fall off the trees into your hand, you got to walk to the store for it. And why do we *walk* to the store for it? Someone in this house, I'll name no names, took the car apart like a clock some years back and left it strewn all down the yard. I've raised auto parts in my garden ten years come Thursday. Ten more years and all that's left of our car is little heaps of rust. Look out that window! It's leaf-raking-and-burning time. It's chopping-trees-and-sawing-wood-for-the-fire time. It's clean-out-stoves-and-hang-storm-doors-and-windows times. It's shingle-the-roof-time, *that's* what it is, and if you think you're out to escape it, think again!"

He placed his hand to his chest. "It pains me you have so little trust in my natural sensitivity to oncoming Doom."

"It pains *me* that *National Geographics* fall in the hands of crazy old men. I see you read those pages then fall into those dreams I always have to sweep up after. Those *Geographic* and *Popular Mechanics* publishers should be forced to see all the half-finished rowboats, helicopters, and one-man batwing gliders in our attic, garage, and cellar. Not only *see,* but cart them home!"

"Chatter on," he said. "I stand before you, a white stone sinking in the tides of Oblivion. For God's sake, woman, can't I drag myself off to die in peace?"

"Plenty of time for Oblivion when I find you stone cold across the kindling pile."

"Jesting Pilate!" he said. "Is recognition of one's own mortality nothing but vanity?"

"You're chewing it like a plug of tobacco."

"Enough!" he said. "My earthly goods are stacked on the back porch. Give them to the Salvation Army."

"The *Geographics* too?"

"Yes, damn it, the *Geographics!* Now stand aside!"

"If you're going to die, you won't need that suitcase full of clothing," she said.

"Hands off, woman! It may take some few hours. Am I to be stripped of my last creature comforts? This should be a tender scene of parting. Instead—bitter recriminations, sarcasm, doubt strewn to every wind."

"All right," she said. "Go spend a cold night in the woods."

"I'm not necessarily going to the woods."

"Where else is there for a man in Illinois to go to die?"

"Well," he said and paused. "Well, there's always the open highway."

"And be run down, of course; I'd forgotten that."

"No, no!" He squeezed his eyes shut, then opened them again. "The empty side roads leading nowhere, everywhere, through night forests, wilderness, to distant lakes. . . ."

"Now, you're not going to go rent a canoe, are you, and

paddle off? Remember the time you tipped over and almost drowned at Fireman's Pier?"

"Who said anything about canoes?"

"You did! Pagan islanders, you said, paddling off into the great unknown."

"That's the South Seas! Here a man has to strike off on foot to find his natural source, seek his natural end. I might walk north along the Lake Michigan shore, the dunes, the wind, the big breakers there."

"Willie, Willie," she said softly, shaking her head. "Oh, Willie, Willie, what will I do with you?"

He lowered his voice. "Just let me have my head," he said.

"Yes," she said, quietly. "Yes." And tears came to her eyes.

"Now, now," he said.

"Oh, Willie . . ." She looked a long while at him. "Do you really think with all your heart you're not going to live?"

He saw himself reflected, small but perfect, in her eye, and looked away uneasily. "I thought all night about the universal tide that brings man in and takes him out. Now it's morning and good-by."

"Good-by?" She looked as if she'd never heard the word before.

His voice was unsteady. "Of course, if you absolutely insist I stay, Mildred——"

"No!" She braced herself and blew her nose. "You feel what you feel; I can't fight that!"

"You *sure?*" he said.

"You're the one that's sure, Willie," she said. "Get on along now. Take your heavy coat; the nights are cold."

"But——" he said.

She ran and brought his coat and kissed his cheek and drew back quickly before he could enclose her in his bear hug. He stood there working his mouth, gazing at the big armchair by the fire. She threw open the front door. "You got food?"

"I won't need . . ." He paused. "I got a boiled ham sandwich and some pickles in my case. Just one. That's all I figured I'd . . ."

And then he was out the door and down the steps and

along the path toward the woods. He turned and was going to say something but thought better of it, waved, and went on.

"Now, Will," she called. "Don't overdo. Don't make too much distance the first hour! You get tired, sit down! You get hungry, eat! And . . ."

But here she had to stop and turn away and get out her handkerchief.

A moment later she looked up the path and it looked as though nobody had passed there in the last ten thousand years. It was so empty she had to go in and shut the door.

Nighttime, nine o'clock, nine-fifteen, stars out, moon round, house lights strawberry-colored through the curtains, the chimney blowing long comet tails of fireworks, sighing warm. Down the chimney, sounds of pots and pans and cutlery, fire on the hearth, like a great orange cat. In the kitchen, the big iron cookstove full of jumping flames, pans boiling, bubbling, frying, vapors and steams in the air. From time to time the old woman turned and her eyes listened and her mouth listened, wide, to the world outside this house, this fire, and this food.

Nine-thirty and, from a great distance away from the house, a solid whacking, chunking sound.

The old woman straightened up and laid down a spoon.

Outside, the dull solid blows came again and again in the moonlight. The sound went on for three or four minutes, during which she hardly moved except to tighten her mouth or her fists with each solid chunking blow. When the sounds stopped, she threw herself at the stove, the table, stirring, pouring, lifting, carrying, setting down.

She finished just as new sounds came from the dark land outside the windows. Footsteps came slowly up the path, heavy shoes weighed the front porch.

She went to the door and waited for a knock.

None came.

She waited a full minute.

Outside on the porch a great bulk stirred and shifted from side to side uneasily.

Finally she sighed and called sharply at the door. "Will, is that you breathing out there?"

No answer. Only a kind of sheepish silence behind the door.

She snatched the door wide.

The old man stood there, an incredible stack of cordwood in his arm. His voice came from behind the stack. "Saw smoke in the chimney; figured you might need wood," he said.

She stood aside. He came in and placed the wood carefully by the hearth, not looking at her.

She looked out on the porch and picked up the suitcase and brought it in and shut the door.

She saw him sitting at the dinner table.

She stirred the soup on the stove to a great boiling whirl.

"Roast beef in the oven?" he asked quietly.

She opened the oven door. The steam breathed across the room to wrap him up. He closed his eyes, seated there, bathed.

"What's that other smell, the burning?" he asked a moment later.

She waited, back turned, and finally said, *"National Geographics."*

He nodded slowly, saying nothing.

Then the food was on the table, warm and tremulous, and there was a moment of silence after she sat down and looked at him. She shook her head. She looked at him. Then she shook her head again silently.

"Do you want to ask the blessing?" she said.

"You," he said.

They sat there in the warm room by the bright fire and bowed their heads and closed their eyes. She smiled and began.

"Thank you, Lord . . ."

All
Summer
in
a
Day

"Ready?"

"Ready."

"Now?"

"Soon."

"Do the scientists really know? Will it happen today, will it?"

"Look, look; see for yourself!"

The children pressed to each other like so many roses, so many weeds, intermixed, peering out for a look at the hidden sun.

It rained.

It had been raining for seven years; thousands upon thousands of days compounded and filled from one end to the other with rain, with the drum and gush of water, with the sweet crystal fall of showers and the concussion of storms so heavy they were tidal waves come over the islands. A thousand forests had been crushed under the rain and grown up a thousand times to be crushed again. And this was the way life was forever on the planet Venus, and this was the schoolroom of the children of the rocket men and women who had come to a raining world to set up civilization and live out their lives.

"It's stopping, it's stopping!"

"Yes, yes!"

Margot stood apart from them, from these children who could never remember a time when there wasn't rain and rain and rain. They were all nine years old, and if there had been a day, seven years ago, when the sun came out for an hour and showed its face to the stunned world, they could not recall. Sometimes, at night, she heard them stir, in remembrance, and she knew they were dreaming and remembering gold or a yellow crayon or a coin large enough to buy the world with. She knew they thought they remembered a warmness, like a blushing in the face, in the body, in the arms and legs and trembling hands. But then they always awoke to the tatting drum, the endless shaking down of clear bead necklaces upon the roof, the walk, the gardens, the forests, and their dreams were gone.

All day yesterday they had read in class about the sun. About how like a lemon it was, and how hot. And they had written small stories or essays or poems about it:

> *I think the sun is a flower,*
> *That blooms for just one hour.*

That was Margot's poem, read in a quiet voice in the still classroom while the rain was falling outside.

"Aw, you didn't write that!" protested one of the boys.

"I did," said Margot. "I did."

"William!" said the teacher.

But that was yesterday. Now the rain was slackening, and the children were crushed in the great thick windows.

"Where's teacher?"

"She'll be back."

"She'd better hurry, we'll miss it!"

They turned on themselves, like a feverish wheel, all tumbling spokes.

Margot stood alone. She was a very frail girl who looked as if she had been lost in the rain for years and the rain had washed out the blue from her eyes and the red from her mouth and the yellow from her hair. She was an old photograph dusted from an album, whitened away, and if she spoke at all her voice would be a ghost.

Now she stood, separate, staring at the rain and the loud wet world beyond the huge glass.

"What're *you* looking at?" said William.

Margot said nothing.

"Speak when you're spoken to." He gave her a shove. But she did not move; rather she let herself be moved only by him and nothing else.

They edged away from her, they would not look at her. She felt them go away. And this was because she would play no games with them in the echoing tunnels of the underground city. If they tagged her and ran, she stood blinking after them and did not follow. When the class sang songs about happiness and life and games her lips barely moved. Only when they sang about the sun and the summer did her lips move as she watched the drenched windows.

And then, of course, the biggest crime of all was that she had come here only five years ago from Earth, and she remembered the sun and the way the sun was and the sky was when she was four in Ohio. And they, they had been on Venus all their lives, and they had been only two years old when last the sun came out and had long since forgotten the color and heat of it and the way it really was. But Margot remembered.

"It's like a penny," she said once, eyes closed.

"No it's not!" the children cried.

"It's like a fire," she said, "in the stove."

"You're lying, you don't remember!" cried the children.

But she remembered and stood quietly apart from all of them and watched the patterning windows. And once, a month ago, she had refused to shower in the school shower rooms, had clutched her hands to her ears and over her head, screaming the water mustn't touch her head. So after that, dimly, dimly, she sensed it, she was different and they knew her difference and kept away.

There was talk that her father and mother were taking her back to Earth next year; it seemed vital to her that they do so, though it would mean the loss of thousands of dollars to her family. And so, the children hated her for all these reasons of big and little consequence. They hated her pale snow face, her waiting silence, her thinness, and her possible future.

"Get away!" The boy gave her another push. "What're you waiting for?"

Then, for the first time, she turned and looked at him. And what she was waiting for was in her eyes.

"Well, don't wait around here!" cried the boy savagely. "You won't see nothing!"

Her lips moved.

"Nothing!" he cried. "It was all a joke, wasn't it?" He turned to the other children. "Nothing's happening today. *Is* it?"

They all blinked at him and then, understanding, laughed and shook their heads. "Nothing, nothing!"

"Oh, but," Margot whispered, her eyes helpless. "But this is the day, the scientists predict, they say, they *know*, the sun . . ."

"All a joke!" said the boy, and seized her roughly. "Hey, everyone, let's put her in a closet before teacher comes!"

"No," said Margot, falling back.

They surged about her, caught her up and bore her, protesting, and then pleading, and then crying, back into a tunnel, a room, a closet, where they slammed and locked the door. They stood looking at the door and saw it tremble from her beating and throwing herself against it. They heard her muffled cries. Then, smiling, they turned and went out and back down the tunnel, just as the teacher arrived.

"Ready, children?" She glanced at her watch.

"Yes!" said everyone.

"Are we all here?"

"Yes!"

The rain slackened still more.

They crowded to the huge door.

The rain stopped.

It was as if, in the midst of a film concerning an avalanche, a tornado, a hurricane, a volcanic eruption, something had, first, gone wrong with the sound apparatus, thus muffling and finally cutting off all noise, all of the blasts and repercussions and thunders, and then, second, ripped the film from the projector and inserted in its place a peaceful tropical slide which did not move or tremor. The world ground to a standstill. The silence was so immense and unbelievable that you felt your ears had been stuffed or you had lost your hearing altogether. The children put their hands to their ears. They stood apart. The door slid back and the smell of the silent, waiting world came in to them.

The sun came out.

It was the color of flaming bronze and it was very large. And the sky around it was a blazing blue tile color. And the jungle burned with sunlight as the children, released from their spell, rushed out, yelling, into the springtime.

"Now, don't go too far," called the teacher after them. "You've only two hours, you know. You wouldn't want to get caught out!"

But they were running and turning their faces up to the sky and feeling the sun on their cheeks like a warm iron; they were taking off their jackets and letting the sun burn their arms.

"Oh, it's better than the sun lamps, isn't it?"

"Much, much better!"

They stopped running and stood in the great jungle that covered Venus, that grew and never stopped growing, tumultuously, even as you watched it. It was a nest of octopi, clustering up great arms of fleshlike weed, wavering, flowering in this brief spring. It was the color of rubber and ash, this jungle, from the many years without sun. It was the color of stones and white cheeses and ink, and it was the color of the moon.

The children lay out, laughing, on the jungle mattress, and heard it sigh and squeak under them, resilient and alive. They ran among the trees, they slipped and fell, they pushed each other, they played hide-and-seek and tag, but most of all they squinted at the sun until tears ran down their faces, they put their hands up to that yellowness and that amazing blueness and they breathed of the fresh, fresh air and listened and listened to the silence which suspended them in a blessed sea of no sound and no motion. They looked at everything and savored everything. Then, wildly, like animals escaped from their caves, they ran and ran in shouting circles. They ran for an hour and did not stop running.

And then——

In the midst of their running one of the girls wailed.

Everyone stopped.

The girl, standing in the open, held out her hand.

"Oh, look, look," she said, trembling.

They came slowly to look at her opened palm.

In the center of it, cupped and huge, was a single raindrop.

She began to cry, looking at it.

They glanced quietly at the sky.

"Oh. Oh."

A few cold drops fell on their noses and their cheeks and their mouths. The sun faded behind a stir of mist. A wind blew cool around them. They turned and started to walk back toward the underground house, their hands at their sides, their smiles vanishing away.

A boom of thunder startled them and like leaves before a new hurricane, they tumbled upon each other and ran. Lightning struck ten miles away, five miles away, a mile, a half mile. The sky darkened into midnight in a flash.

They stood in the doorway of the underground for a moment until it was raining hard. Then they closed the door and heard the gigantic sound of the rain falling in tons and avalanches, everywhere and forever.

"Will it be seven more years?"

"Yes. Seven."

Then one of them gave a little cry.

"Margot!"

"What?"

"She's still in the closet where we locked her."

"Margot."

They stood as if someone had driven them, like so many stakes, into the floor. They looked at each other and then looked away. They glanced out at the world that was raining now and raining and raining steadily. They could not meet each other's glances. Their faces were solemn and pale. They looked at their hands and feet, their faces down.

"Margot."

One of the girls said, "Well . . . ?"

No one moved.

"Go on," whispered the girl.

They walked slowly down the hall in the sound of cold rain. They turned through the doorway to the room in the sound of the storm and thunder, lightning on their faces, blue and terrible. They walked over to the closet door slowly and stood by it.

Behind the closet door was only silence.

They unlocked the door, even more slowly, and let Margot out.

The
Gift

Tomorrow would be Christmas, and even while the three of them rode to the rocket port the mother and father were worried. It was the boy's first flight into space, his very first time in a rocket, and they wanted everything to be perfect. So when, at the custom's table, they were forced to leave behind his gift which exceeded the weight limit by no more than a few ounces and the little tree with the lovely white candles, they felt themselves deprived of the season and their love.

The boy was waiting for them in the Terminal room. Walking toward him, after their unsuccessful clash with the Interplanetary officials, the mother and father whispered to each other.

"What shall we do?"

"Nothing, nothing. What *can* we do?"

"Silly rules!"

"And he so wanted the tree!"

The siren gave a great howl and people pressed forward into the Mars Rocket. The mother and father walked at the very last, their small pale son between them, silent.

"I'll think of something," said the father.

"What . . . ?" asked the boy.

And the rocket took off and they were flung headlong into dark space.

138

The rocket moved and left fire behind and left Earth behind on which the date was December 24, 2052, heading out into a place where there was no time at all, no month, no year, no hour. They slept away the rest of the first "day." Near midnight, by their Earth-time New York watches, the boy awoke and said, "I want to go look out the porthole."

There was only one port, a "window" of immensely thick glass of some size, up on the next deck.

"Not quite yet," said the father. "I'll take you up later."

"I want to see where we are and where we're going."

"I want you to wait for a reason," said the father.

He had been lying awake, turning this way and that, thinking of the abandoned gift, the problem of the season, the lost tree and the white candles. And at last, sitting up, no more than five minutes ago, he believed he had found a plan. He need only carry it out and this journey would be fine and joyous indeed.

"Son," he said, "in exactly one half hour it will be Christmas."

"Oh," said the mother, dismayed that he had mentioned it. Somehow she had rather hoped that the boy would forget.

The boy's face grew feverish and his lips trembled. "I know, I know. Will I get a present, will I? Will I have a tree? You promised——"

"Yes, yes, all that, and more," said the father.

The mother started. "But——"

"I mean it," said the father. "I really mean it. All and more, much more. Excuse me, now. I'll be back."

He left them for about twenty minutes. When he came back he was smiling. "Almost time."

"Can I hold your watch?" asked the boy, and the watch was handed over and he held it ticking in his fingers as the rest of the hour drifted by in fire and silence and unfelt motion.

"It's Christmas *now!* Christmas! Where's my present?"

"Here we go," said the father and took his boy by the shoulder and led him from the room, down the hall, up a rampway, his wife following.

"I don't understand," she kept saying.

"You will. Here we are," said the father.

They had stopped at the closed door of a large cabin. The father tapped three times and then twice in a code. The door opened and the light in the cabin went out and there was a whisper of voices.

"Go on in, son," said the father.

"It's dark."

"I'll hold your hand. Come on, Mama."

They stepped into the room and the door shut, and the room was very dark indeed. And before them loomed a great glass eye, the porthole, a window four feet high and six feet wide, from which they could look out into space.

The boy gasped.

Behind him the father and the mother gasped with him, and then in the dark room some people began to sing.

"Merry Christmas, son," said the father.

And the voices in the room sang the old, the familiar carols, and the boy moved forward slowly until his face was pressed against the cool glass of the port. And he stood there for a long long time, just looking and looking out into space and the deep night at the burning and the burning of ten billion billion white and lovely candles. . . .

The
Great
Collision
of
Monday
Last

The man staggered through the flung-wide doors of Heber
Finn's pub as if struck by lightning. Reeling, blood on his
face, coat, and torn pants, his moan froze every customer
at the bar. For a time you heard only the soft foam
popping in the lacy mugs, as the customers turned, some
faces pale, some pink, some veined and wattle-red. Every
eyelid down the line gave a blink.

The stranger swayed in his ruined clothes, eyes wide,
lips trembling. The drinkers clenched their fist. Yes! they
cried, silently—go on, man! what *happened?*

The stranger leaned far out on the air.

"Collision," he whispered. "Collision on the road."

Then, chopped at the knees, he fell.

"Collision!" A dozen men rushed at the body.

"Kelly!" Heber Finn vaulted the bar. "Get to the road!
Mind the victim; easy does it! Joe, run for the Doc!"

"Wait!" said a quiet voice.

From the private stall at the dark end of the pub, the
cubby where a philosopher might brood, a dark man
blinked out at the crowd.

"Doc!" cried Heber Finn. "It's you!"

Doctor and men hustled out into the night.

"Collision . . ." The man on the floor twitched his lips.

"Softly, boys." Heber Finn and two others gentled the

141

victim atop the bar. He looked handsome as death on the fine inlaid wood with the prismed mirror making him two dread calamities for the price of one.

Outside on the steps, the crowd halted, shocked as if an ocean had sunk Ireland in the dusk and now bulked all about them. Fog in fifty-foot rollers and breakers put out the moon and stars. Blinking, cursing, the men leapt out to vanish in the deeps.

Behind, in the bright doorframe, a young man stood. He was neither red enough nor pale enough of face, nor dark enough or light enough in spirit to be Irish, and so must be American. He was. That established, it follows he dreaded interfering with what seemed village ritual. Since arriving in Ireland, he could not shake the feeling that at all times he was living stage center of the Abbey Theatre. Now, not knowing his lines, he could only stare after the rushing men.

"But," he protested weakly, "I didn't hear any cars on the road."

"You did not!" said an old man almost pridefully. Arthritis limited him to the top step where he teetered, shouting at the white tides where his friends had submerged. "Try the crossroad, boys! That's where it most often does!"

"The crossroad!" Far and near, footsteps rang.

"Nor," said the American, "did I hear a collision."

The old man snorted with contempt. "Ah, we don't be great ones for commotion, nor great crashing sounds. But collision you'll see if you step on out there. Walk, now, don't run! It's the devil's own night. Running blind you might hit into Kelly, beyond, who's a great one for running just to squash his lungs. Or you might head on with Feeney, too drunk to find any road, never mind what's *on* it! You got a torch, a flash? Blind you'll be, but use it. Walk now, you *hear?*"

The American groped through the fog to his car, found his flashlight, and, immersed in the night beyond Heber Finn's, made direction by the heavy clubbing of shoes and a rally of voices ahead. A hundred yards off in eternity the men approached, grunting whispers: "Easy now!" "Ah, the shameful blight!" "Hold on, don't jiggle him!"

The American was flung aside by a steaming lump of

men who swept suddenly from the fog, bearing atop themselves a crumpled object. He glimpsed a blood-stained and
livid face high up there, then someone cracked his flashlight down.

By instinct, sensing the far whiskey-colored light of
Heber Finn's, the catafalque surged on toward that fixed
and familiar harbor.

Behind came dim shapes and a chilling insect rattle.

"Who's that!" cried the American.

"Us, with the vehicles," someone husked. "You might
say—we got the collision."

The flashlight fixed them. The American gasped. A moment later, the battery failed.

But not before he had seen two village lads jogging
along with no trouble at all, easily, lightly, toting under
their arms two ancient black bicycles minus front and
tail lights.

"What . . . ?" said the American.

But the lads trotted off, the accident with them. The
fog closed in. The American stood abandoned on an empty
road, his flashlight dead in his hand.

By the time he opened the door at Heber Finn's, both
"bodies" as they called them, had been stretched on the
bar.

"We got the bodies on the bar," said the old man, turning as the American entered.

And there was the crowd lined up not for drinks, but
blocking the way so the Doc had to shove sidewise from
one to another of these relics of blind driving by
night on the misty roads.

"One's Pat Nolan," whispered the old man. "Not working at the moment. The other's Mr. Peevey from Meynooth, in candy and cigarettes mostly." Raising his voice,
"Are they dead now, Doc?"

"Ah, be still, won't you?" The Doc resembled a sculptor
troubled at finding some way to finish up two full-length
marble statues at once. "Here, let's put one victim on the
floor!"

"The floor's a tomb," said Heber Finn. "He'll catch his
death down there. Best leave him up where the warm air
gathers from our talk."

"But," said the American quietly, confused, "I've never

heard of an accident like this in all my life. Are you sure there were absolutely no cars? Only these two men on their *bikes?*"

"Only!" The old man shouted. "Great God, man, a fellow working up a drizzling sweat can pump along at sixty kilometers. With a long downhill glide his bike hits ninety or ninety-five! So here they come, these two, no front or tail lights——"

"Isn't there a law against that?"

"To hell with government interference! So here the two come, no lights, flying home from one town to the next. Thrashing like Sin Himself's at their behinds! Both going opposite ways but both on the same side of the road. Always ride the wrong side of the road, it's safer, they say. But look on these lads, fair destroyed by all that official palaver. Why? Don't you see? One remembered it, but the other didn't! Better if the officials kept their mouths shut! For here the two be, dying."

"Dying?" The American stared.

"Well, think on it, man! What stands between two able-bodied hell-bent fellas jumping along the path from Kilcock to Meynooth? Fog! Fog is all! Only fog to keep their skulls from bashing together. Why, look when two chaps hit at a cross like that, it's like a strike in bowling alleys, tenpins flying! Bang! There go your friends, nine feet up, heads together like dear chums met, flailing the air, their bikes clenched like two tomcats. Then they all fall down and just lay there, feeling around for the Dark Angel."

"Surely these men won't——"

"Oh, won't they? Why, last year alone in all the Free State no night passed some soul did not meet in fatal collision with another!"

"You mean to say over three hundred Irish bicyclists die every year, hitting each other?"

"God's truth and a pity."

"I never ride my bike nights." Heber Finn eyed the bodies. "I walk."

"But still then the damn bikes run you down!" said the old man. "Awheel or afoot, some idiot's always panting up Doom the other way. They'd sooner split you down the seam than wave hello. Oh, the brave men I've seen ruined or half-ruined or worse, and headaches their life-

times after." The old man trembled his eyelids shut.
"You might almost think, mightn't you, that human beings
was not made to handle such delicate instruments of
power."

"Three hundred dead each year." The American seemed
dazed.

"And that don't count the 'walking wounded' by the
thousands every fortnight who, cursing, throw their bikes
in the bog forever and take government pensions to
salve their all-but-murdered bodies."

"Should we stand here talking?" The American gestured
helplessly toward the victims. "Is there a hospital?"

"On a night with no moon," Heber Finn continued,
"best walk out through the middle of fields and be damned
to the evil roads! That's how I have survived into this
my fifth decade."

"Ah . . ." The men stirred restlessly.

The Doc, sensing he had withheld information too
long, feeling his audience drift away, now snatched their
attention back by straightening up briskly and exhaling.

"Well!"

The pub quickened into silence.

"This chap here——" The Doc pointed. "Bruises, lac-
erations, and agonizing backaches for two weeks running.
As for the other lad, however——" And here the Doc
let himself scowl for a long moment at the paler one
there looking rouged, waxed, and ready for final rites.
"Concussion."

"Concussion!"

The quiet wind rose and fell in the silence.

"He'll survive if we run him quick now to Meynooth
Clinic. So whose car will volunteer?"

The crowd turned as a staring body toward the American. He felt the gentle shift as he was drawn from outside the ritual to its deep and innermost core. He flushed,
remembering the front of Heber Finn's pub, where seventeen bicycles and one automobile were parked at this
moment. Quickly, he nodded.

"There! A volunteer, lads! Quick now, hustle this boy
—gently!—to our good friend's vehicle!"

The men reached out to lift the body, but froze when the
American coughed. They saw him circle his hand to all,

and tip his cupped fingers to his lips. They gasped in soft surprise. The gesture was not done when drinks foamed down the bar.

"For the road!"

And now even the luckier victim, suddenly revived, face like cheese, found a mug gentled to his hand with whispers.

"Here, lad, here . . . tell us . . ."

". . . what happened, eh? eh?"

Then the body was gone off the bar, the potential wake over, the room empty save for the American, the Doc, the revived lad, and two softly cudgeling friends. Outside you could hear the crowd putting the one serious result of the great collision into the volunteer's car.

The Doc said, "Finish your drink, Mr.——?"

"McGuire," said the American.

"By the saints, he's Irish!"

No, thought the American, far away, looking numbly around at the pub, at the recovered bicyclist seated, waiting for the crowd to come back and mill about him, seeing the blood-spotted floor, the two bicycles tilted near the door like props from a vaudeville turn, the dark night waiting outside with its improbable fog, listening to the roll and cadence and gentle equilibrium of these voices balanced each in its own throat and environment. No, thought the American named McGuire, I'm almost, but certainly not quite, Irish. . . .

"Doctor," he heard himself say as he placed money on the bar, "do you often have auto wrecks, collisions, between people in *cars?*"

"Not in our town!" The Doc nodded scornfully east. "If you like that sort of thing, now, Dublin's the very place for it!"

Crossing the pub together, the Doc took his arm as if to impart some secret which would change his Fates. Thus steered, the American found the stout inside himself a shifting weight he must accommodate from side to side as the Doc breathed soft in his ear.

"Look here now, McGuire, admit it, you've driven but little in Ireland, right? Then, listen! Driving to Meynooth, fog and all, you'd best take it fast! Raise a din! Why?

Scare the cyclists and cows off the path, both sides! If you drive slow, why you'll creep up on and do away with dozens before they know what took them off! And another thing: when a car approaches, douse your lights! Pass each other, lights out, in safety. Them devil's own lights have put out more eyes and demolished more innocents than all of seeing's worth. Is it clear, now? Two things: speed, and douse your lights when cars loom up!"

At the door, the American nodded. Behind him he heard the one victim, settled easy in his chair, working the stout around on his tongue, thinking, preparing, beginning his tale:

"Well, I'm on me way home, blithe as you please, asailing downhill near the cross when——"

Outside in the car with the other collision victim moaning softly in the back seat, the Doc offered final advice.

"Always wear a cap, lad. If you want to walk nights ever, on the roads, that is. A cap'll save you the frightful migraines should you meet Kelly or Moran or any other hurtling full-tilt the other way, full of fiery moss and hard-skulled from birth. Even on foot, these men are dangerous. So you see, there's rules for pedestrians too in Ireland, and wear a cap at night is Number One!"

Without thinking, the American fumbled under the seat, brought forth a brown tweed cap purchased in Dublin that day, and put it on. Adjusting it, he looked out at the dark mist boiling across the night. He listened to the empty highway waiting for him ahead, quiet, quiet, quiet, but not quiet somehow. For hundreds of long strange miles up and down all of Ireland he saw a thousand crossroads covered with a thousand fogs through which one thousand tweed-capped, grey-mufflered phantoms wheeled along in mid-air, singing, shouting, and smelling of Guiness Stout.

He blinked. The phantoms shadowed off. The road lay empty and dark and waiting.

Taking a deep breath, shutting his eyes, the American named McGuire turned the key in the switch and stepped on the starter.

The
Little
Mice

"They're very odd," I said. "The little Mexican couple."

"How do you mean?" asked my wife.

"Never a sound," I said. "Listen."

Ours was a house deep back in among tenements, to which another half house had been added. When my wife and I purchased the house, we rented the additional quarters which lay walled up against one side of our parlor. Now, listening at this particular wall, we heard our hearts beat.

"I know they're home," I whispered. "But in the three years they've lived here I've never heard a dropped pan, a spoken word, or the sound of a light switch. Good God, what are they *doing* in there?"

"I'd never thought," said my wife. "It *is* peculiar."

"Only one light on, that same dim little blue twenty-five-watt bulb they burn in their parlor. If you walk by and peer in their front door, there *he* is, sitting in his armchair, not saying a word, his hands in his lap. There she is, sitting in the other armchair, looking at him, saying nothing. They don't move."

"At first glance I always think they're not home," said my wife. "Their parlor's so dark. But if you stare long enough, your eyes get used to it and you can make them out, sitting there."

148

"Some day," I said, "I'm going to run in, turn on their lights, and yell! My God, if *I* can't stand their silence, how can they? They can talk, can't they?"

"When he pays the rent each month, he says hello."

"What else?"

"Good-by."

I shook my head. "When we meet in the alley he smiles and runs."

My wife and I sat down for an evening of reading, the radio, and talk. "Do they have a radio?"

"No radio, television, telephone. Not a book, magazine, or paper in their house."

"Ridiculous!"

"Don't get so excited."

"I know, but you can't sit in a dark room two or three years and not speak, not listen to a radio, not read or even eat, can you? I've never smelled a steak or an egg frying. Damn it, I don't believe I've ever heard them go to bed!"

"They're doing it to mystify us, dear."

"They're succeeding!"

I went for a walk around the block. It was a nice summer evening. Returning, I glanced idly in their front door. The dark silence was there, and the heavy shapes, sitting, and the little blue light burning. I stood a long time, finishing my cigarette. It was only in turning to go that I saw him in the doorway, looking out with his bland, plump face. He didn't move. He just stood there, watching me.

"Evening," I said.

Silence. After a moment, he turned, moving away into the dark room.

In the morning, the little Mexican left the house at seven o'clock, alone, hurrying down the alley, observing the same silence he kept in his rooms. She followed at eight o'clock, walking carefully, all lumpy under her dark coat, a black hat balanced on her frizzy, beauty-parlor hair. They had gone to work this way, remote and silent, for years.

"Where do they work?" I asked at breakfast.

"He's a blast-furnace man at U. S. Steel here. She sews in a dress loft somewhere."

"That's hard work."

I typed a few pages of my novel, read, idled, typed some more. At five in the afternoon I saw the little Mexican woman come home, unlock her door, hurry inside, hook the screen, and lock the door tight.

He arrived at six sharp in a rush. Once on their back porch, however, he became infinitely patient. Quietly, raking his hand over the screen, lightly, like a fat mouse scrabbling, he waited. At last she let him in. I did not see their mouths move.

Not a sound during suppertime. No frying. No rattle of dishes. Nothing.

I saw the small blue lamp go on.

"That's how he is," said my wife, "when he pays the rent. Raps so quietly I don't hear. I just happen to glance out the window and there he is. God knows how long he's waited, standing, sort of 'nibbling' at the door."

Two nights later, on a beautiful July evening, the little Mexican man came out on the back porch and looked at me, working in the garden and said, "You're crazy!" He turned to my wife. "You're crazy too!" He waved his plump hand quietly. "I don't like you. Too much *noise*. I don't like you. You're crazy."

He went back into his little house.

August, September, October, November. The "mice," as we now referred to them, lay quietly in their dark nest. Once my wife gave him some old magazines with his rent receipt. He accepted these politely, with a smile and a bow, but no word. An hour later she saw him put the magazines in the yard incinerator and strike a match.

The next day he paid the rent three months in advance, no doubt figuring that he would only have to see us up close once every twelve weeks. When I saw him on the street he crossed quickly to the other side to greet an imaginary friend. She, similarly, ran by me, smiling wildly, bewildered, nodding. I never got nearer than twenty yards to her. If there was plumbing to be fixed in their house, they went silently forth on their own, not telling us, and brought back a plumber who worked, it seemed, with a flashlight.

"God damnedest thing," he told me when I saw him in the alley. "Damn fool place there hasn't got any light bulbs in the sockets. When I asked where they all were, damn it, they just *smiled* at me!"

I lay at night thinking about the little mice. Where were they from? Mexico, yes. What part? A farm, a small village, somewhere by a river? Certainly no city or town. But a place where there were stars and the normal lights and darkness, the goings and comings of the moon and the sun they had known the better part of their lives. Yet here they were, far, far away from home, in an impossible city, he sweating out the hell of blast furnaces all day, she bent to jittering needles in a sewing loft. They came home then to this block, through a loud city, avoided clanging streetcars and saloons that screamed like red parrots along their way. Through a million shriekings they ran back to their parlor, their blue light, their comfortable chairs, and their silence. I often thought of this. Late at night I felt if I put out my hand, in the dark of my own bedroom, I might feel adobe and hear a cricket and a river running by under the moon and someone singing softly to a faint guitar.

Late one December evening the next-door tenement burned. Flames roared at the sky, bricks fell in avalanches, and sparks littered the roof where the quiet mice lived.

I pounded their door.

"Fire!" I cried. "Fire!"

They sat motionless in their blue-lighted room.

I pounded violently. "You *hear?* Fire!"

The fire engines arrived. They gushed water into the tenement. More bricks fell. Four of them smashed holes in the little house. I climbed to the roof, extinguished the small fires there, and scrambled down, my face dirty and my hands cut. The door to the little house opened. The quiet little Mexican and his wife stood in the doorway, solid and unmoved.

"Let me in!" I cried. "There's a hole in your roof; some sparks may have fallen in your bedroom!"

I pulled the door wide, pushed past them.

"No!" the little man grunted.

"Ah!" the little woman ran in a circle like a broken toy.

I was inside with a flashlight. The little man seized my arm.

I smelled his breath.

And then my flashlight shot through the rooms of their house. Light sparkled on a hundred wine bottles standing in the hall, two hundred bottles shelved in the kitchen, six dozen along the parlor wallboards, more of the same on bedroom bureaus and in closets. I do not know if I was more impressed with the hole in the bedroom ceiling or the endless glitter of so many bottles. I lost count. It was like an invasion of gigantic shining beetles, struck dead, deposited, and left by some ancient disease.

In the bedroom I felt the little man and woman behind me in the doorway. I heard their loud breathing and I could feel their eyes. I raised the beam of my flashlight away from the glittering bottles, I focused it carefully, and for the rest of my visit, on the hole in the yellow ceiling.

The little woman began to cry. She cried softly. Nobody moved.

The next morning they left.

Before we even knew they were going, they were half down the alley at 6 A.M., carrying their luggage, which was light enough to be entirely empty. I tried to stop them. I talked to them. They were old friends, I said. Nothing had changed, I said. They had nothing to do with the fire, I said, or the roof. They were innocent bystanders, I *insisted!* I would fix the roof myself, no charge, no charge to them! But they did not look at me. They looked at the house and at the open end of the alley ahead of them while I talked. Then, when I stopped they nodded to the alley as if agreeing that it was time to go, and walked off, and then began to run, it seemed, away from me, toward the street where there were streetcars and buses and automobiles and many loud avenues stretching in a maze. They hurried proudly, though, heads up, not looking back.

It was only by accident I ever met them again. At Christmas time, one evening, I saw the little man running quietly along the twilight street ahead of me. On a personal whim I followed. When he turned, I turned. At last, five blocks away from our old neighborhood, he scratched quietly at the door of a little white house. I saw the door open, shut, and lock him in. As night settled over the tenement city, a small light burned like blue mist in the tiny living room as I passed. I thought I saw, but probably imagined, two silhouettes there, he on his side of the room in his own particular chair, and she on her side of the room, sitting, sitting in the dark, and one or two bottles beginning to collect on the floor behind the chairs, and not a sound, not a sound between them. Only the silence.

I did not go up and knock. I strolled by. I walked on along the avenue, listening to the parrot cafés scream. I bought a newspaper, a magazine, and a quarter-edition book. Then I went home to where all the lights were lit and there was warm food upon the table.

The
Shore
Line
at
Sunset

Tom, knee-deep in the waves, a piece of driftwood in his hand, listened.

The house, up toward the Coast Highway in the late afternoon, was silent. The sounds of closets being rummaged, suitcase locks snapping, vases being smashed, and of a final door crashing shut, all had faded away.

Chico, standing on the pale sand, flourished his wire strainer to shake out a harvest of lost coins. After a moment, without glancing at Tom, he said, "Let her go."

So it was every year. For a week or a month, their house would have music swelling from the windows, there would be new geraniums potted on the porch rail, new paint on the doors and steps. The clothes on the wire line changed from harlequin pants to sheath dresses to hand-made Mexican frocks like white waves breaking behind the house. Inside, the paintings on the walls shifted from imitation Matisse to pseudo-Italian Renaissance. Sometimes, looking up, he would see a woman drying her hair like a bright yellow flag on the wind. Sometimes the flag was black or red. Sometimes the woman was tall, sometimes short, against the sky. But there was never more than one woman at a time. And, at last, a day like today came. . . .

Tom placed his driftwood on the growing pile near

where Chico sifted the billion footprints left by people long vanished from their holidays.

"Chico. What are we doing here?"

"Living the life of Reilly, boy!"

"I don't feel like Reilly, Chico."

"Work at it, boy!"

Tom saw the house a month from now, the flowerpots blowing dust, the walls hung with empty squares, only sand carpeting the floors. The rooms would echo like shells in the wind. And all night every night bedded in separate rooms he and Chico would hear a tide falling away and away down a long shore, leaving no trace.

Tom nodded, imperceptibly. Once a year he himself brought a nice girl here, knowing she was right at last and that in no time they would be married. But his women always stole silently away before dawn, feeling they had been mistaken for someone else, not being able to play the part. Chico's friends left like vacuum cleaners, with a terrific drag, roar, rush, leaving no lint unturned, no clam unprized of its pearl, taking their purses with them like toy dogs which Chico had petted as he opened their jaws to count their teeth.

"That's four women so far this year."

"Okay, referee." Chico grinned. "Show me the way to the showers."

"Chico——" Tom bit his lower lip, then went on. "I been thinking. Why don't we split up?"

Chico just looked at him.

"I mean," said Tom, quickly, "maybe we'd have better luck, alone."

"Well, I'll be goddamned," said Chico slowly, gripping the strainer in his big fists before him. "Look here, boy, don't you know the facts? You and me, we'll be here come the year 2000. A couple of crazy dumb old gooney-birds drying their bones in the sun. Nothing's ever going to happen to us now, Tom, it's too late. Get that through your head and shut up."

Tom swallowed and looked steadily at the other man. "I'm thinking of leaving—next week."

"Shut up, shut up, and get to work!"

Chico gave the sand an angry showering rake that tilled him forty-three cents in dimes, pennies, and nickels. He

stared blindly at the coins shimmering down the wires
like a pinball game all afire.

Tom did not move, holding his breath.

They both seemed to be waiting for something.

The something happened.

"Hey . . . hey . . . hey . . ."

From a long way off down the coast a voice called.

The two men turned slowly.

"Hey . . . hey . . . oh, hey . . . !"

A boy was running, yelling, waving, along the shore
two hundred yards away. There was something in his
voice that made Tom feel suddenly cold. He held onto his
own arms, waiting.

"Hey!"

The boy pulled up, gasping, pointing back along the
shore.

"A woman, a funny woman, by the North Rock!"

"A woman!" The words exploded from Chico's mouth
and he began to laugh. "Oh, no, no!"

"What you mean, a 'funny' woman?" asked Tom.

"I don't know," cried the boy, his eyes wide. "You got
to come see! Awful funny!"

"You mean 'drowned'?"

"Maybe! She came out of the water, she's lying on the
shore, you got to see, yourself . . . funny . . ." The boy's
voice died. He gazed off north again. "She's got a fish's
tail."

Chico laughed. "Not before supper, please."

"Please!" cried the boy, dancing now. "No lie! Oh,
hurry!"

He ran off, sensed he was not followed, and looked
back in dismay.

Tom felt his lips move. "Boy wouldn't run this far for
a joke, would he, Chico?"

"People have run further for less."

Tom started walking. "All right, son."

"Thanks, mister, oh thanks!"

The boy ran. Twenty yards up the coast, Tom looked
back. Behind him, Chico squinted, shrugged, dusted his
hands wearily, and followed.

They moved north along the twilight beach, their skin
weathered in tiny folds about their burnt pale eyes, look-

ing younger for their hair cut close to the skull so you could not see the grey. There was a fair wind and the ocean rose and fell with prolonged concussions.

"What," said Tom, "what if we get to North Rock and it's true? The ocean *has* washed some *thing* up?"

But before Chico could answer, Tom was gone, his mind racing down coasts littered with horseshoe crabs, sand dollars, starfish, kelp, and stone. From all the times he'd talked on what lives in the sea, the names returned with the breathing fall of waves. Argonauts, they whispered, codlings, pollacks, houndfish, tautog, tench, sea elephant, they whispered, gillings, flounders, and beluga, the white whale, and grampus, the sea dog . . . always you thought how these must look from their deep-sounding names. Perhaps you would never in your life see them rise from the salt meadows beyond the safe limits of the shore, but they were there, and their names, with a thousand others, made pictures. And you looked and wished you were a frigate-bird that might fly nine thousand miles around to return some year with the full size of the ocean in your head.

"Oh, quick!" The boy had run back to peer in Tom's face. "It might be gone!"

"Keep your shirt on, boy," said Chico.

They came around the North Rock. A second boy stood there, looking down.

Perhaps from the corner of his eye, Tom saw something on the sand that made him hesitate to look straight at it, but fix instead on the face of the boy standing there. The boy was pale and he seemed not to breathe. On occasion he remembered to take a breath, his eyes focused, but the more they saw there on the sand the more they took time off from focusing and turned blank and looked stunned. When the ocean came in over his tennis shoes, he did not move or notice.

Tom glanced away from the boy to the sand.

And Tom's face, in the next moment, became the face of the boy. His hands assumed the same curl at his sides and his mouth moved to open and stay half open and his eyes, which were light in color, seemed to bleach still more with so much looking.

The setting sun was ten minutes above the sea.

"A big wave came in and went out," said the first boy, "and here she was."

They looked at the woman lying there.

Her hair was very long and it lay on the beach like the threads of an immense harp. The water stroked along the threads and floated them up and let them down, each time in a different fan and silhouette. The hair must have been five or six feet long and now it was strewn on the hard wet sand and it was the color of limes.

Her face . . .

The men bent half down in wonder.

Her face was white sand sculpture, with a few water drops shimmering on it like summer rain upon a cream-colored rose. Her face was that moon which when seen by day is pale and unbelievable in the blue sky. It was milk-marble veined with faint violet in the temples. The eyelids, closed down upon the eyes, were powdered with a faint water color, as if the eyes beneath gazed through the fragile tissue of the lids and saw them standing there above her, looking down and looking down. The mouth was a pale flushed sea-rose, full and closed upon itself. And her neck was slender and white and her breasts were small and white, now covered, uncovered, covered, uncovered in the flow of water, the ebb of water, the flow, the ebb, the flow. And the breasts were flushed at their tips, and her body was startlingly white, almost an illumination, a white-green lightning against the sand. And as the water shifted her, her skin glinted like the surface of a pearl.

The lower half of her body changed itself from white to very pale blue, from very pale blue to pale green, from pale green to emerald green, to moss and lime green, to scintallas and sequins all dark green, all flowing away in a fount, a curve, a rush of light and dark, to end in a lacy fan, a spread of foam and jewel on the sand. The two halves of this creature were so joined as to reveal no point of fusion where pearl woman, woman of a whiteness made of cream-water and clear sky merged with that half which belonged to the amphibious slide and rush of current that came up on the shore and shelved down the shore, tugging its half toward its proper home. The woman was the sea, the sea was woman.

There was no flaw or seam, no wrinkle or stitch; the illusion, if illusion it was, held perfectly together and the blood from one moved into and through and mingled with what must have been the ice waters of the other.

"I wanted to run get help." The first boy seemed not to want to raise his voice. "But Skip said she was dead and there's no help for that. Is she?"

"She was never alive," said Chico. "Sure," he went on, feeling their eyes on him suddenly. "It's something left over from a movie studio. Liquid rubber skinned over a steel frame. A prop, a dummy."

"Oh, no, it's real!"

"We'll find a label somewhere," said Chico. "Here."

"Don't!" cried the first boy.

"Hell." Chico touched the body to turn it, and stopped. He knelt there, his face changing.

"What's the matter?" asked Tom.

Chico took his hand away and looked at it. "I was wrong." His voice faded.

Tom took the woman's wrist. "There's a pulse."

"You're feeling your own heartbeat."

"I just don't know . . . maybe . . . maybe . . ."

The woman was there and her upper body was all moon pearl and tidal cream and her lower body all slithering ancient green-black coins that slid upon themselves in the shift of wind and water.

"There's a trick somewhere!" cried Chico, suddenly.

"No. No!" Just as suddenly Tom burst out in laughter. "No trick! My God, my God, I feel great! I haven't felt so great since I was a kid!"

They walked slowly around her. A wave touched her white hand so the fingers faintly softly waved. The gesture was that of someone asking for another and another wave to come in and lift the fingers and then the wrist and then the arm and then the head and finally the body and take all of them together back down out to sea.

"Tom." Chico's mouth opened and closed. "Why don't you go get our truck?"

Tom didn't move.

"You hear me?" said Chico.

"Yes, but——"

"But what? We could sell this somewhere, I don't

know—the university, that aquarium at Seal Beach or . . . well, hell, why couldn't we just set up a place? Look." He shook Tom's arm. "Drive to the pier. Buy us three hundred pounds of chipped ice. When you take anything out of the water you *need* ice, don't you?"

"I never thought."

"Think about it! Get moving!"

"I don't know, Chico."

"What you mean? She's real, isn't she?" He turned to the boys. "*You* say she's real, don't you? Well, then, what are we waiting for?"

"Chico," said Tom. "You better go get the ice your-self."

"Someone's got to stay and make sure she don't go back out with the tide!"

"Chico," said Tom. "I don't know how to explain. I don't want to get that ice for you."

"I'll go myself, then. Look, boys, build the sand up here to keep the waves back. I'll give you five bucks apiece. Hop to it!"

The sides of the boys' faces were bronze-pink from the sun which was touching the horizon now. Their eyes were a bronze color looking at Chico.

"My God!" said Chico. "This is better than finding ambergris!" He ran to the top of the nearest dune, called, "Get to work!" and was gone.

Now Tom and the two boys were left with the lonely woman by the North Rock and the sun was one-fourth of the way below the western horizon. The sand and the woman were pink-gold.

"Just a little line," whispered the second boy. He drew his fingernail along under his own chin, gently. He nodded to the woman. Tom bent again to see the faint line under either side of her firm white chin, the small, almost invisible line where the gills were or had been and were now almost sealed shut, invisible.

He looked at the face and the great strands of hair spread out in a lyre on the shore.

"She's beautiful," he said.

The boys nodded without knowing it.

Behind them, a gull leaped up quickly from the dunes. The boys gasped and turned to stare.

Tom felt himself trembling. He saw the boys were trembling too. A car horn hooted. Their eyes blinked, suddenly afraid. They looked up toward the highway.

A wave poured about the body, framing it in a clear white pool of water.

Tom nodded the boys to one side.

The wave moved the body an inch in and two inches out toward the sea.

The next wave came and moved the body two inches in and six inches out toward the sea.

"But——" said the first boy.

Tom shook his head.

The third wave lifted the body two feet down toward the sea. The wave after that drifted the body another foot down the shingles and the next three moved it six feet down.

The first boy cried out and ran after it.

Tom reached him and held his arm. The boy looked helpless and afraid and sad.

For a moment there were no more waves. Tom looked at the woman, thinking, she's true, she's real, she's mine . . . but . . . she's dead. Or will be if she stays here.

"We can't let her go," said the first boy. "We can't, we just can't!"

The other boy stepped between the woman and the sea. "What would we do with her?" he wanted to know, looking at Tom, "if we kept her?"

The first boy tried to think. "We could—we could——" He stopped and shook his head. "Oh, my Gosh."

The second boy stepped out of the way and left a path from the woman to the sea.

The next wave was a big one. It came in and went out and the sand was empty. The whiteness was gone and the black diamonds and the great threads of the harp.

They stood by the edge of the sea, looking out, the man and the two boys, until they heard the truck driving up on the dunes behind them.

The last of the sun was gone.

They heard footsteps running on the dunes and someone yelling.

They drove back down the darkening beach in the light truck with the big treaded tires in silence. The two boys sat in the rear on the bags of chipped ice. After a long while, Chico began to swear steadily, half to himself, spitting out the window.

"Three hundred pounds of ice. Three hundred *pounds* of ice! What do I do with it now? And I'm soaked to the skin, soaked! You didn't even move when I jumped in and swam out to look around! Idiot, idiot! You haven't changed! Like every other time, like always, you do nothing, nothing, just stand there, stand there, do nothing, nothing, just stare!"

"And what did you do, I ask, what?" said Tom, in a tired voice, looking ahead. "The same as you always did, just the same, no different, no different at all. You should've seen yourself."

They dropped the boys off at their beach house. The youngest spoke in a voice you could hardly hear against the wind. "Gosh, nobody'll ever believe . . ."

The two men drove down the coast and parked.

Chico sat for two or three minutes waiting for his fists to relax on his lap, and then he snorted.

"Hell. I guess things turn out for the best." He took a deep breath. "It just came to me. Funny. Twenty, thirty years from now, middle of the night, our phone'll ring. It'll be one of those two boys, grown-up, calling long-distance from a bar somewhere. Middle of the night, them calling to ask one question. It's *true*, isn't it? they'll say. It *did* happen, didn't it? Back in 1958, it really happened to *us*? And we'll sit there on the edge of the bed, middle of the night, saying, Sure, boy, sure, it really happened to us in 1958. And they'll say, Thanks, and we'll say, Don't mention it, any old time. And we'll all say good night. And maybe they won't call again for a couple of years."

The two men sat on their front-porch steps in the dark.

"Tom?"

"What?"

Chico waited a moment.

"Tom, next week—you're not going away."

It was not a question but a quiet statement.

Tom thought about it, his cigarette dead in his fingers.

And he knew that now he could never go away. For tomorrow and the day after the day after that he would walk down and go swimming there in all the green and white fires and the dark caverns in the hollows under the strange waves. Tomorrow and tomorrow and tomorrow.

"Yes, Chico. I'm staying here."

Now the silver looking glasses advanced in a crumpling line all along the coast from a thousand miles north to a thousand miles south. The mirrors did not reflect so much as one building or one tree or one highway or one car or even one man himself. The mirrors reflected only the quiet moon and then shattered into a billion bits of glass that spread out in a glaze on the shore. Then the sea was dark awhile, preparing another line of mirrors to rear up and surprise the two men who sat there for a long time never once blinking their eyes, waiting.

*The
Strawberry
Window*

In his dream he was shutting the front door with its strawberry windows and lemon windows and windows like
white clouds and windows like clear water in a country
stream. Two dozen panes squared round the one big
pane, colored of fruit wines and gelatins and cool water
ices. He remembered his father holding him up as a
child. "Look!" And through the green glass the world
was emerald, moss, and summer mint. "Look!" The lilac
pane made livid grapes of all the passers-by. And at last
the strawberry glass perpetually bathed the town in
roseate warmth, carpeted the world in pink sunrise, and
made the cut lawn seem imported from some Persian rug
bazaar. The strawberry window, best of all, cured people
of their paleness, warmed the cold rain, and set the blowing, shifting February snows afire.

"Yes, yes! There——!"

He awoke.

He heard his boys talking before he was fully out of
his dream and he lay in the dark now, listening to the
sad sound their talk made, like the wind blowing the
white sea-bottoms into the blue hills, and then he remembered.

We're on Mars, he thought.

"What?" His wife cried out in her sleep.

He hadn't realized he had spoken; he lay as still as he possibly could. But now, with a strange kind of numb reality, he saw his wife rise to haunt the room, her pale face staring through the small, high windows of their quonset hut at the clear but unfamiliar stars.

"Carrie," he whispered.

She did not hear.

"Carrie," he whispered. "There's something I want to tell you. For a month now I've been wanting to say . . . tomorrow . . . tomorrow morning, there's going to be . . ."

But his wife sat all to herself in the blue starlight and would not look at him.

If only the sun stayed up, he thought, if only there was no night. For during the day he nailed the settlement town together, the boys were in school, and Carrie had cleaning, gardening, cooking to do. But when the sun was gone and their hands were empty of flowers or hammers and nails and arithmetics, their memories, like night birds, came home in the dark.

His wife moved, a slight turn of her head.

"Bob," she said at last, "I want to go home."

"Carrie!"

"This isn't home," she said.

He saw that her eyes were wet and brimming. "Carrie, hold on awhile."

"I've got no fingernails from holding on now!"

As if she still moved in her sleep, she opened her bureau drawers and took out layers of handkerchiefs, shirts, underclothing, and put it all on top of the bureau, not seeing it, letting her fingers touch and bring it out and put it down. The routine was long familiar now. She would talk and put things out and stand quietly awhile, and then later put all the things away and come, dry-faced, back to bed and dreams. He was afraid that some night she would empty every drawer and reach for the few ancient suitcases against the wall.

"Bob . . ." Her voice was not bitter, but soft, featureless, and as uncolored as the moonlight that showed what she was doing. "So many nights for six months I've talked this way; I'm ashamed. You work hard building houses in town. A man who works so hard shouldn't have to listen to a wife gone sad on him. But there's nothing to

do but talk it out. It's the little things I miss most of all.
I don't know—silly things. Our front-porch swing. The
wicker rocking chair, summer nights. Looking at the people walk or ride by those evenings, back in Ohio. Our
black upright piano, out of tune. My Swedish cut glass.
Our parlor furniture—oh, it was like a herd of elephants,
I know, and all of it old. And the Chinese hanging
crystals that hit when the wind blew. And talking to
neighbors there on the front porch, July nights. All those
crazy, silly things . . . they're not important. But it
seems those are things that come to mind around three
in the morning. I'm sorry."

"Don't be," he said. "Mars is a far place. It smells
funny, looks funny, and feels funny. I think to myself
nights too. We came from a nice town."

"It was green," she said. "In the spring and summer.
And yellow and red in the fall. And ours was a nice
house; my, it was old, eighty–ninety years or so. Used
to hear the house talking at night, whispering away. All
the dry wood, the banisters, the front porch, the sills.
Wherever you touched, it talked to you. Every room a
different way. And when you had the whole house talking, it was a family around you in the dark, putting you
to sleep. No other house, the kind they build nowadays,
can be the same. A lot of people have got to go through
and live in a house to make it mellow down all over.
This place here, now, this hut, it doesn't know I'm in it,
doesn't care if I live or die. It makes a noise like tin,
and tin's cold. It's got no pores for the years to sink in.
It's got no cellar for you to put things away for next
year and the year after that. It's got no attic where you
keep things from last year and all the other years before you were born. If we only had a little bit up here
that was familiar, Bob, then we could make room for
all that's strange. But when everything, *every single thing*
is strange, then it takes forever to make things familiar."

He nodded in the dark. "There's nothing you say that
I haven't thought."

She was looking at the moonlight where it lay upon the
suitcases against the wall. He saw her move her hand
down toward them.

"Carrie!"

"What?"

He swung his legs out of bed. "Carrie, I've done a crazy damn-fool thing. All these months I heard you dreaming away, scared, and the boys at night and the wind, and Mars out there, the sea-bottoms and all, and . . ." He stopped and swallowed. "You got to understand what I did and why I did it. All the money we had in the bank a month ago, all the money we saved for ten years, I spent."

"Bob!"

"I threw it away, Carrie, I swear, I threw it away on nothing. It was going to be a surprise. But now, tonight, there you are, and there are those damned suitcases on the floor and . . ."

"Bob," she said, turning around. "You mean we've gone through all *this,* on Mars, putting away extra money every week, only to have you burn it up in a few hours?"

"I don't know," he said. "I'm a crazy fool. Look, it's not long till morning. We'll get up early. I'll take you down to see what I've done. I don't want to tell you, I want you to see. And if it's no go, then, well, there's always those suitcases and the rocket to Earth four times a week."

She did not move. "Bob, Bob," she murmured.

"Don't say any more," he said.

"Bob, Bob . . ." She shook her head slowly, unbelievingly. He turned away and lay back down on his own side of the bed, and she sat on the other side, and for a moment did not lie down, but only sat looking at the bureau where her handkerchiefs and jewelry and clothing lay ready in neat stacks where she had left them. Outside a wind the color of moonlight stirred up the sleeping dust and powdered the air.

At last she lay back, but said nothing more and was a cold weight in the bed, staring down the long tunnel of night toward the faintest sign of morning.

They got up in the very first light and moved in the small quonset hut without a sound. It was a pantomime prolonged almost to the time when someone might scream at the silence, as the mother and father and the boys washed and dressed and ate a quiet breakfast of toast and fruit juice and coffee, with no one looking directly at anyone and everyone watching someone in the reflective surfaces of toaster, glassware, or cutlery, where all their faces were melted out of shape and made terribly alien in the early hour. Then, at last, they opened the quonset door and let in the air that blew across the cold blue-white Martian seas, where only the sand tides dissolved and shifted and made ghost patterns, and they stepped out under a raw and staring cold sky and began their walk toward a town, which seemed no more than a motion-picture set far on ahead of them on a vast, empty stage.

"What part of town are we going to?" asked Carrie.

"The rocket depot," he said. "But before we get there, I've a lot to say."

The boys slowed down and moved behind their parents, listening. The father gazed ahead, and not once in all the time he was talking did he look at his wife or sons to see how they were taking all that he said.

"I believe in Mars," he began quietly. "I guess I believe some day it'll belong to us. We'll nail it down. We'll settle in. We won't turn tail and run. It came to me one day a year ago, right after we first arrived. Why did we come? I asked myself. Because, I said, because. It's the same thing with the salmon every year. The salmon don't know why they go where they go, but they go, anyway. Up rivers they don't remember, up streams, jumping waterfalls, but finally making it to where they propagate and die, and the whole thing starts again. Call it racial memory, instinct, call it nothing, but there it is. And here we are."

They walked in the silent morning with the great sky watching them and the strange blue and steam-white sands sifting about their feet on the new highway.

"So here we are. And from Mars where? Jupiter, Neptune, Pluto, and on out? Right. *And on out.* Why? Some day the sun will blow up like a leaky furnace. Boom—there goes Earth. But maybe Mars won't be hurt; or if Mars is hurt maybe Pluto won't be, or if Pluto's hurt, then where'll *we* be, our sons' sons, that is?"

He gazed steadily up into that flawless shell of plum-colored sky.

"Why, we'll be on some world with a number maybe;

planet 6 of star system 97, planet 2 of system 99! So damn far off from here you need a nightmare to take it in! We'll be gone, do you see, gone off away and safe! And I thought to myself, ah, ah. So that's the reason we came to Mars, so *that's* the reason men shoot off their rockets."

"Bob——"

"Let me finish; not to make money, no. Not to see the sights, no. Those are the lies men tell, the fancy reasons they give themselves. Get rich, get famous, they say. Have fun, jump around, they say. But all the while, inside, something else is ticking along the way it ticks in salmon or whales, the way it ticks, by God, in the smallest microbe you want to name. And that little clock that ticks in everything living, you know what it says? It says get away, spread out, move along, keep swimming. Run to so many worlds and build so many towns that *nothing* can ever kill man. You *see*, Carrie? It's not just us come to Mars, it's the race, the whole darn human race, depending on how *we* make out in our lifetime. This thing is so big I want to laugh, I'm so scared stiff of it."

He felt the boys walking steadily behind him and he felt Carrie beside him and he wanted to see her face and how she was taking all this, but he didn't look there, either.

"All this is no different than me and Dad walking the fields when I was a boy, casting seed by hand when our seeder broke down and we'd no money to fix it. It had to be done, somehow, for the later crops. My God, Carrie, my God, you *remember* those Sunday-supplement articles, THE EARTH WILL FREEZE IN A MILLION YEARS! I bawled once, as a boy, reading articles like that. My mother asked why. I'm bawling for all those poor people up ahead, I said. Don't worry about them, Mother said. But, Carrie, that's my whole point; we *are* worrying about them. Or we wouldn't be here. It matters if Man with a capital M keeps going. There's nothing better than Man with a capital M in my books. I'm prejudiced, of course, because I'm one of the breed. But if there's any way to get hold of that immortality men are always talking about, this is the way—spread out—seed the universe. Then you got a harvest against crop failures anywhere down the line. No matter if Earth has famines or the rust comes in. You got the new wheat lifting on Venus or

where-in-hell-ever man gets to in the next thousand
years, I'm crazy with the idea, Carrie, crazy. When I
finally hit on it I got so excited I wanted to grab people,
you, the boys, and tell them. But hell, I knew that wasn't
necessary. I knew a day or night would come when you'd
hear that ticking in yourselves too, and then you'd see,
and no one'd have to say anything again about all this. It's
big talk, Carrie, I know, and big thoughts for a man just
short of five feet five, but by all that's holy, it's true."

They moved through the deserted streets of the town
and listened to the echoes of their walking feet.

"And this morning?" said Carrie.

"I'm coming to this morning," he said. "Part of *me*
wants to go home too. But the other part says if we go,
everything's lost. So I thought, what bothers us most?
Some of the things we once had. Some of the boys' things,
your things, mine. And I thought, if it takes an old thing
to get a new thing started, by God, I'll use the old thing.
I remember from history books that a thousand years ago
they put charcoals in a hollowed out cow horn, blew on
them during the day, so they carried their fire on marches
from place to place, to start a fire every night with the
sparks left over from morning. Always a new fire, but
always something of the old in it. So I weighed and balanced it off. Is the Old worth all our money? I asked. No!
It's only the things we *did* with the Old that have any
worth. Well, then, is the New worth *all* our money? I
asked. Do you feel like investing in the day after the middle of next week? Yes! I said. If I can fight this thing that
makes us want to go back to Earth, I'd dip my money
in kerosene and strike a match!"

Carrie and the two boys did not move. They stood on
the street, looking at him as if he were a storm that had
passed over and around, almost blowing them from the
ground, a storm that was now dying away.

"The freight rocket came in this morning," he said,
quietly. "Our delivery's on it. Let's go and pick it up."

They walked slowly up the three steps into the rocket
depot and across the echoing floor toward the freight
room that was just sliding back its doors, opening for
the day.

"Tell us again about the salmon," said one of the boys.

In the middle of the warm morning they drove out of town in a rented truck filled with great crates and boxes and parcels and packages, long ones, tall ones, short ones, flat ones, all numbered and neatly addressed to one Robert Prentiss, New Toledo, Mars.

They stopped the truck by the quonset hut and the boys jumped down and helped their mother out. For a moment Bob sat behind the wheel, and then slowly got out himself to walk around and look into the back of the truck at the crates.

And by noon all but one of the boxes were opened and their contents placed on the sea-bottom where the family stood among them.

"Carrie . . ."

And he led her up the old porch steps that now stood uncrated on the edge of town.

"Listen to 'em, Carrie."

The steps squeaked and whispered underfoot.

"What do they say, tell me what they say?"

She stood on the ancient wooden steps, holding to herself, and could not tell him.

He waved his hand. "Front porch here, living room there, dining room, kitchen, three bedrooms. Part we'll build new, part we'll bring. Of course all we got here now is the front porch, some parlor furniture, and the old bed."

"All that money, Bob!"

He turned, smiling. "You're not mad, now, look at me! You're not mad. We'll bring it all up, next year, five years! The cut-glass vases, that Armenian carpet your mother gave us in 1961! Just *let* the sun explode!"

They looked at the other crates, numbered and lettered: Front-porch swing, front-porch wicker rocker, hanging Chinese crystals . . .

"I'll blow them myself to make them ring."

They set the front door, with its little panes of colored glass, on the top of the stairs, and Carrie looked through the strawberry window.

"What do you see?"

But he knew what she saw, for he gazed through the colored glass, too. And there was Mars, with its cold sky warmed and its dead seas fired with color, with its hills like mounds of strawberry ice, and its sand like burning charcoals sifted by wind. The strawberry window, the strawberry window, breathed soft rose colors on the land and filled the mind and the eye with the light of a never-ending dawn. Bent there, looking through, he heard himself say:

"The town'll be out this way in a year. This'll be a shady street, you'll have your porch, and you'll have friends. You won't *need* all this so much, then. But starting right here, with this little bit that's familiar, watch it spread, watch Mars change so you'll know it as if you've known it all your life."

He ran down the steps to the last and as-yet unopened canvas-covered crate. With his pocket knife he cut a hole in the canvas. "Guess!" he said.

"My kitchen stove? My furnace?"

"Not in a million years." He smiled very gently. "Sing me a song," he said.

"Bob, you're clean off your head."

"Sing me a song worth all the money we had in the bank and now don't have, but who gives a blast in hell," he said.

"I don't know anything but 'Genevieve, Sweet Gene-vieve!' "

"Sing that," he said.

But she could not open her mouth and start the song. He saw her lips move and try, but there was no sound.

He ripped the canvas wider and shoved his hand into the crate and touched around for a quiet moment, and started to sing the words himself until he moved his hand a last time and then a single clear piano chord sprang out on the morning air.

"There," he said. "Let's take it right on to the end. Everyone! Here's the harmony."

The
Day
It
Rained
Forever

The hotel stood like a hollowed dry bone under the very center of the desert sky where the sun burned the roof all day. All night, the memory of the sun stirred in every room like the ghost of an old forest fire. Long after dusk, since light meant heat, the hotel lights stayed off. The inhabitants of the hotel preferred to feel their way blind through the halls in their never-ending search for cool air.

This one particular evening Mr. Terle, the proprietor, and his only boarders, Mr. Smith and Mr. Fremley, who looked and smelled like two ancient rags of cured tobacco, stayed late on the long veranda. In their creaking glockenspiel rockers they gasped back and forth in the dark, trying to rock up a wind.

"Mr. Terle . . . ? Wouldn't it be *really* nice . . . someday . . . if you could buy . . . air conditioning . . . ?"

Mr. Terle coasted awhile, eyes shut.

"Got no money for such things, Mr. Smith."

The two old boarders flushed; they hadn't paid a bill now in twenty-one years.

Much later Mr. Fremley sighed a grievous sigh. "Why, why don't we all just quit, pick up, get outa here, move to a decent city? Stop this swelterin' and fryin' and sweatin'."

"Who'd buy a dead hotel in a ghost town?" said Mr.

173

Terle quietly. "No. No, we'll just set here and wait, wait for that great day, January 29."

Slowly, all three men stopped rocking.

January 29.

The one day in all the year when it really let go and rained.

"Won't wait long." Mr. Smith tilted his gold railroad watch like the warm summer moon in his palm. "Two hours and nine minutes from now it'll *be* January 29. But I don't see nary a cloud in ten thousand miles."

"It's rained every January 29 since I was born!" Mr. Terle stopped, surprised at his own loud voice. "If it's a day late this year, I won't pull God's shirttail."

Mr. Fremley swallowed hard and looked from east to west across the desert toward the hills. "I wonder . . . will there ever be a gold rush hereabouts again?"

"No gold," said Mr. Smith. "And what's more, I'll make you a bet—no rain. No rain tomorrow or the day after the day after tomorrow. No rain all the rest of this year."

The three old men sat staring at the big sun-yellowed moon that burned a hole in the high stillness.

After a long while, painfully, they began to rock again.

The first hot morning breezes curled the calendar pages like a dried snake skin against the flaking hotel front.

The three men, thumbing their suspenders up over their hat rack shoulders, came barefoot downstairs to blink out at that idiot sky.

"January 29 . . ."

"Not a drop of mercy there."

"Day's young."

"*I'm* not." Mr. Fremley turned and went away.

It took him five minutes to find his way up through the delirious hallways to his hot, freshly baked bed.

At noon, Mr. Terle peered in.

"Mr. Fremley . . . ?"

"Damn desert cactus, that's us!" gasped Mr. Fremley, lying there, his face looking as if at any moment it might fall away in a blazing dust on the raw plank floor. "But even the best damn cactus got to have just a sip of water before it goes back to another year of the same damn furnace. I tell you I won't move again, I'll lie here an' die if I don't hear more than birds pattin' around up on that roof!"

"Keep your prayers simple and your umbrella handy," said Mr. Terle and tiptoed away.

At dusk, on the hollow roof a faint pattering sounded. Mr. Fremley's voice sang out mournfully from his bed.

"Mr. Terle, that ain't rain! That's you with the garden hose sprinklin' well water on the roof! Thanks for tryin', but cut it out, now."

The pattering sound stopped. There was a sigh from the yard below.

Coming around the side of the hotel a moment later, Mr. Terle saw the calendar fly out and down in the dust.

"Damn January 29!" cried a voice. "Twelve more months! Have to wait twelve more months, now!"

Mr. Smith was standing there in the doorway. He stepped inside and brought out two dilapidated suitcases and thumped them on the porch.

"Mr. Smith!" cried Mr. Terle. "You can't leave after thirty years!"

"They say it rains twenty days a month in Ireland," said Mr. Smith. "I'll get a job there and run around with my hat off and my mouth open."

"You can't go!" Mr. Terle tried frantically to think of something; he snapped his fingers. "You owe me nine thousand dollars rent!"

Mr. Smith recoiled; his eyes got a look of tender and unexpected hurt in them.

"I'm sorry." Mr. Terle looked away. "I didn't mean that. Look now—you just head for Seattle. Pours two inches a week there. Pay me when you can, or never. But do me a favor: wait till midnight. It's cooler then, anyhow. Get you a good night's walk toward the city."

"Nothin'll happen between now and midnight."

"You got to have faith. When everything else is gone, you got to believe a thing'll happen. Just stand here with me, you don't have to sit, just stand here and think of rain. That's the last thing I'll ever ask of you."

On the desert sudden little whirlwinds of dust twisted up, sifted down. Mr. Smith's eyes scanned the sunset horizon.

"What do I think? Rain, oh you rain, come along here? Stuff like that?"

"Anything. Anything at all!"

Mr. Smith stood for a long time between his two mangy suitcases and did not move. Five, six minutes ticked by. There was no sound, save the two men's breathing in the dusk.

Then at last, very firmly, Mr. Smith stooped to grasp the luggage handles.

Just then, Mr. Terle blinked. He leaned forward, cupping his hand to his ear.

Mr. Smith froze, his hands still on the luggage.

From away among the hills, a murmur, a soft and tremulous rumble.

"Storm coming!" hissed Mr. Terle.

The sound grew louder; a kind of whitish cloud rose up from the hills.

Mr. Smith stood tall on tiptoe.

Upstairs Mr. Fremley sat up like Lazarus.

Mr. Terle's eyes grew wider and yet wider to take hold of what was coming. He held to the porch rail like the captain of a calm-foundered vessel feeling the first stir of some tropic breeze that smelled of lime and the ice-cool white meat of coconut. The smallest wind stroked over his aching nostrils as over the flues of a white-hot chimney.

"There!" cried Mr. Terle. "There!"

And over the last hill, shaking out feathers of fiery dust, came the cloud, the thunder, the racketing storm.

Over the hill the first car to pass in twenty days flung itself down the valley with a shriek, a thud, and a wail.

Mr. Terle did not dare to look at Mr. Smith.

Mr. Smith looked up, thinking of Mr. Fremley in his room.

Mr. Fremley, at the window, looked down and saw the car expire and die in front of the hotel.

For the sound that the car made was curiously final. It had come a very long way on blazing sulphur roads, across salt flats abandoned ten million years ago by the shingling off of waters. Now, with wire-ravelings like cannibal hair sprung up from seams, with a great eyelid of canvas top thrown back and melted to spearmint gum over the rear seat, the auto, a Kissel car, vintage 1924, gave a final shuddering as if to expel its ghost upon the air.

The old woman in the front seat of the car waited patiently, looking in at the three men and the hotel as if to say, Forgive me, my friend is ill; I've known him a long while, and now I must see him through his final hour. So she just sat in the car waiting for the faint convulsions to cease and for the great relaxation of all the bones which signifies that the final process is over. She must have sat a full half minute longer listening to her car, and there was something so peaceful about her that Mr. Terle and Mr. Smith leaned slowly toward her. At last she looked at them with a grave smile and raised her hand.

Mr. Fremley was surprised to see his hand go out the window, above and wave back to her.

On the porch Mr. Smith murmured, "Strange. It's not a storm. And I'm not disappointed. How come?"

But Mr. Terle was down the path and to the car.

"We thought you were . . . that is . . ." He trailed off. "Terle's my name, Joe Terle."

She took his hand and looked at him with absolutely clear and unclouded light blue eyes like water that has melted from snow a thousand miles off and come a long way, purified by wind and sun.

"Miss Blanche Hillgood," she said, quietly. "Graduate of the Grinnell College, unmarried teacher of music, thirty years high-school glee club and student orchestra conductor, Green City, Iowa, twenty years private teacher of piano, harp, and voice, one month retired and living on a pension and now, taking my roots with me, on my way to California."

"Miss Hillgood, you don't look to be going anywhere from here."

"I had a feeling about that." She watched the two men circle the car cautiously. She sat like a child on the lap of a rheumatic grandfather, undecided. "Is there nothing we can do?"

"Make a fence of the wheels, dinner gong of the brake drums, the rest'll make a fine rock garden."

Mr. Fremley shouted from the sky. "Dead? I say, is

the car dead? I can *feel* it from here! Well—it's way past time for supper!"

Mr. Terle put out his hand. "Miss Hillgood, that there is Joe Terle's Desert Hotel, open twenty-six hours a day. Gila monsters and road runners please register before going upstairs. Get you a night's sleep, free, we'll knock our Ford off its blocks and drive you to the city come morning."

She let herself be helped from the car. The machine groaned as if in protest at her going. She shut the door carefully with a soft click.

"One friend gone, but the other still with me. Mr. Terle, could you please bring her in out of the weather?"

"Her, ma'am?"

"Forgive me, I never think of things but what they're people. The car was a man, I suppose, because it took me places. But a harp, now, don't you agree, is female?"

She nodded to the rear seat of the car. There, tilted against the sky like an ancient scrolled leather ship prow cleaving the wind, stood a case which towered above any driver who might sit up in front and sail the desert calms or the city traffics.

"Mr. Smith," said Mr. Terle, "lend a hand."

They untied the huge case and hoisted it gingerly out between them.

"What you got there?" cried Mr. Fremley from above.

Mr. Smith stumbled. Miss Hillgood gasped. The case shifted in the two men's arms.

From within the case came a faint musical humming.

Mr. Fremley, above, heard. It was all the answer he needed. Mouth open, he watched the lady and the two men and their boxed friend sway and vanish in the cavernous porch below.

"Watch out!" said Mr. Smith. "Some damn fool left his luggage here——" He stopped. "Some damn fool? *Me!*"

The two men looked at each other. They were not perspiring any more. A wind had come up from somewhere, a gentle wind that fanned their shirt collars and flapped the strewn calendar gently in the dust.

"*My* luggage . . ." said Mr. Smith.

Then they all went inside.

"More wine, Miss Hillgood? Ain't had wine on the table in years."

"Just a touch, if you please."

They sat by the light of a single candle which made the room an oven and struck fire from the good silverware and the uncracked plates as they talked and drank warm wine and ate.

"Miss Hillgood, get on with your life."

"All my life," she said, "I've been so busy running from Beethoven to Bach to Brahms, I never noticed I was twenty-nine. Next time I looked up I was forty. Yesterday, seventy-one. Oh, there were men; but they'd given up singing at ten and given up flying when they were twelve. I always figured we were born to fly, one way or other, so I couldn't stand most men shuffling along with all the iron of the earth in their blood. I never met a man who weighed less than nine hundred pounds. In their black business suits, you could hear them roll by like funeral wagons."

"So you flew away?"

"Just in my mind, Mr. Terle. It's taken sixty years to make the final break. All that time I grabbed onto piccolos and flutes and violins because they make streams in the air, you know, like streams and rivers on the ground. I rode every tributary and tried every freshwater wind from Handel on down to a whole slew of Strausses. It's been the far way around that's brought me here."

"How'd you finally make up your mind to leave?" asked Mr. Smith.

"I looked around last week and said, 'Why, look, you've been flying *alone!* No one in all Green City really cares *if* you fly or how high you go. It's always, 'Fine, Blanche,' or 'thanks for the recital at the PTA tea, Miss H.' But no one really listening. And when I talked a long time ago about Chicago or New York, folks swatted me and laughed. 'Why be a little frog in a big pond when you can be the biggest frog in all Green City!' So I stayed on, while the folks who gave me advice moved away or died or both. The rest had wax in their ears. Just last week I shook myself and said, 'Hold on! Since when do *frogs* have wings?' "

"So now you're headin' west?" said Mr. Terle.

"Maybe to play in pictures or in that orchestra under the stars. But somewhere I just must play at last for someone who'll hear and really listen. . . ."

They sat there in the warm dark. She was finished, she had said it all now, foolish or not—and she moved back quietly in her chair.

Upstairs someone coughed.

Miss Hillgood heard, and rose.

It took Mr. Fremley a moment to ungum his eyelids and make out the shape of the woman bending down to place the tray by his rumpled bed.

"What you all talking about down there just now?"

"I'll come back later and tell you word for word," said Miss Hillgood. "Eat now. The salad's fine." She moved to leave the room.

He said, quickly, "You goin' to stay?"

She stopped half out the door and tried to trace the expression on his sweating face in the dark. He, in turn, could not see her mouth or eyes. She stood a moment longer, silently, then went on down the stairs.

"She must not've heard me," said Mr. Fremley.

But he knew she had heard.

Miss Hillgood crossed the downstairs lobby to fumble with the locks on the upright leather case.

"I must pay you for my supper."

"On the house," said Mr. Terle.

"I must pay," she said, and opened the case.

There was a sudden flash of gold.

The two men quickened in their chairs. They squinted at the little old woman standing beside the tremendous heart-shaped object which towered above her with its shining columbined pedestal atop which a calm Grecian face with antelope eyes looked serenely at them even as Miss Hillgood looked now.

The two men shot each other the quickest and most startled of glances, as if each had guessed what might happen next. They hurried across the lobby, breathing hard, to sit on the very edge of the hot velvet lounge, wiping their faces with damp handkerchiefs.

Miss Hillgood drew a chair under her, rested the

golden harp gently back on her shoulder, and put her hands to the strings.

Mr. Terle took a breath of fiery air and waited.

A desert wind came suddenly along the porch outside, tilting the chairs so they rocked this way and that like boats on a pond at night.

Mr. Fremley's voice protested from above. "What's goin' on down there?"

And then Miss Hillgood moved her hands.

Starting at the arch near her shoulder, she played her fingers out along the simple tapestry of wires toward the blind and beautiful stare of the Greek goddess on her column, and then back. Then for a moment she paused and let the sounds drift up through the baked lobby air and into all the empty rooms.

If Mr. Fremley shouted, above, no one heard. For Mr. Terle and Mr. Smith were so busy jumping up to stand riven in the shadows, they heard nothing save the storming of their own hearts and the shocked rush of all the air in their lungs. Eyes wide, mouths dropped, in a kind of pure insanity, they stared at the two women there, the blind Muse proud on her golden pillar, and the seated one, gentle eyes closed, her small hands stretched forth on the air.

Like a girl, they both thought wildly, like a little girl putting her hands out a window to feel what? Why, of course, of course!

To feel the rain.

The echo of the first shower vanished down remote causeways and roof drains, away.

Mr. Fremley, above, rose from his bed as if pulled round by his ears.

Miss Hillgood played.

She played and it wasn't a tune they knew at all, but it was a tune they had heard a thousand times in their long lives, words or not, melody or not. She played and each time her fingers moved, the rain fell pattering through the dark hotel. The rain fell cool at the open windows and the rain rinsed down the baked floor boards of the porch. The rain fell on the roof top and fell on hissing sand, it fell on rusted car and empty stable and dead cactus in the yard. It washed the windows and laid the dust and filled the rain barrels and curtained the doors with beaded threads that might part and whisper as you walked through. But more than anything the soft touch and coolness of it fell on Mr. Smith and Mr. Terle. Its gentle weight and pressure moved them down and down until it had seated them again. By its continuous budding and prickling on their faces it made them shut up their eyes and mouths and raise their hands to shield it away. Seated there, they felt their heads tilt slowly back to let the rain fall where it would.

The flash flood lasted a minute, then faded away as the fingers trailed down the loom, let drop a few last bursts and squalls and then stopped.

The last chord hung in the air like a picture taken when lightning strikes and freezes a billion drops of water on their downward flight. Then the lightning went out. The last drops fell through darkness in silence.

Miss Hillgood took her hands from the strings, her eyes still shut.

Mr. Terle and Mr. Smith opened their eyes to see those two miraculous women way over there across the lobby somehow come through the storm untouched and dry.

They trembled. They leaned forward as if they wished to speak. They looked helpless, not knowing what to do.

And then a single sound from high above in the hotel corridors drew their attention and told them what to do.

The sound came floating down feebly, fluttering like a tired bird beating its ancient wings.

The two men looked up and listened.

It was the sound of Mr. Fremley.

Mr. Fremley, in his room, applauding.

It took five seconds for Mr. Terle to figure out what it was. Then he nudged Mr. Smith and began, himself, to beat his palms together. The two men struck their hands in mighty explosions. The echoes ricocheted around about in the hotel caverns above and below, striking walls, mirrors, windows, trying to fight free of the rooms.

Miss Hillgood opened her eyes now, as if this new storm had come on her in the open, unprepared.

The men gave their own recital. They smashed their hands together so fervently it seemed they had fistfuls of firecrackers to set off, one on another. Mr. Fremley shouted. Nobody heard. Hands winged out, banged shut again and again until fingers puffed up and the old men's breath came short and they put their hands at last on their knees, a heart pounding inside each one.

Then, very slowly, Mr. Smith got up and still looking at the harp, went outside and carried in the suitcases. He stood at the foot of the lobby stairs looking for a long while at Miss Hillgood. He glanced down at her single piece of luggage resting there by the first tread. He looked from her suitcase to her and raised his eyebrows questioningly.

Miss Hillgood looked at her harp, at her suitcase, at Mr. Terle, and at last back to Mr. Smith.

She nodded once.

Mr. Smith bent down and with his own luggage under one arm and her suitcase in the other, he started the long slow climb up the stairs in the gentle dark. As he moved, Miss Hillgood put the harp back on her shoulder and either played in time to his moving or he moved in time to her playing, neither of them knew which.

Half up the flight, Mr. Smith met Mr. Fremley who, in a faded robe, was testing his slow way down.

Both stood there, looking deep into the lobby at the one man on the far side in the shadows, and the two women further over, no more than a motion and a gleam. Both thought the same thoughts.

The sound of the harp playing, the sound of the cool water falling every night and every night of their lives, after this. No spraying the roof with the garden hose now any more. Only sit on the porch or lie in your night bed and hear the falling . . . the falling . . . the falling . . .

Mr. Smith moved on up the stair; Mr. Fremley moved down.

The harp, the harp. Listen, listen!

The fifty years of drought were over.

The time of the long rains had come.

ARTHUR HAILEY

AIRPORT

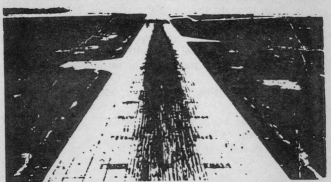

SOON TO BE A MAJOR UNIVERSAL MOTION PICTURE